From New York Times
Harrison comes the exp.
Unseen!

When Dragos and Pia move to the Other land of Rhyacia, they hope starting a new life will bring safety and freedom to their family, especially their young baby, Niall. And at first their new home seems perfect... but looks are deceiving.

Beneath Rhyacia's idyllic façade an ancient, malevolent force lurks, waiting for the right opportunity to break free of its cage. When that opportunity comes, it strikes with devastating accuracy.

While Dragos has never backed down from a fight, he's also never encountered an enemy like this one before. How can he fight a foe who doesn't have a body? A foe who can invade and turn his own mind against him?

How can Dragos protect his family, when at any moment one of them may become the enemy?

As Dragos and Pia race against time to fight this unseen menace, they must also acknowledge a terrifying truth— when anyone can become the enemy, no one can be trusted.

An adversary who can trap the dragon poses a threat to everyone in Rhyacia, and that means no one is safe...

*** This book does NOT end on a cliffhanger ***

The Adversary

Thea Harrison

The Adversary
Copyright © 2021 by Teddy Harrison LLC
ISBN 13: 978-1-947046-34-4
Print Edition

Cover design by Beti Bup at BetiBup33 Studio Design

Prologue

(from *The Unseen*)

"Your husband is dead," the imposter spat. His nose had been bloodied and droplets sprayed Pia's face.

She didn't flinch. Instead she leaned closer and stared into his eyes. "If my husband is dead," she said, "then I have nothing to lose, do I?"

He started to laugh then convulsed. Briefly—oh so briefly—hot gold flashed in his eyes. Dragos snarled telepathically, *Do what you need to do.*

The next minute, Dragos was gone again, and the creature who glared back at her had eyes of amber. It hurt so bad to see him so briefly, yet at the same time triumph swelled. Somehow, somewhere, her mate was still in there.

And she would do whatever she needed to get him back.

"This is going to suck really badly for you," she told the imposter. "Because my husband's body is incredibly strong, and he can survive a lot of abuse." Standing, she avoided looking at Liam. She said to the sentinels who ringed them, "Question him. Do whatever it takes."

Then she walked away. They moved to close the gap behind her, and Dragos disappeared from view.

Chapter One

WALKING AWAY FROM her mate was the hardest thing Pia had ever done. He was still there inside his body, trapped by someone—some *thing*—that was in there with him.

Her hands shook and her vision blurred. Onlookers stood scattered in clumps across the beach, staring with fear and puzzlement written across their faces. She couldn't look at any of them.

Then something happened behind her. No doubt the sentinels were obeying her order, because Dragos let out a muffled groan.

No. That wasn't Dragos. It was the imposter, the thief of everything.

It wasn't Dragos.

But, oh gods, it sure sounded like him.

The Wyr were two-natured, human—or at least human-like—and animal, and the animal that lived inside her turned savage, clawing at her to whirl and attack those who dared threaten and hurt her mate. It didn't understand logic or strategy, or that Dragos was presently infected by a dangerous entity.

After a brief struggle for control, she broke and ran as fast as she could away from the scene.

Eva called out from behind her. "Pia—"

"Not now!" In case anyone chose to disregard her, she picked up speed until she flew across the sand.

Soon she left the lights and sounds of the people behind, and the moon lit her way. There were winged Wyr who were faster than Pia when they took to the air, but nothing on land could catch her when she put her heart and soul into it—as she did now, trying to outrun the horror of that muffled groan.

She had no idea where her baby had been taken. Niall had been hidden away for his own safety, along with the other children in the settlement.

She had no idea how to help her mate. All she could do was run while her heart felt like it was tearing into pieces. When she was far enough away from everybody, she turned from the beach and plunged into the forest. There, surrounded by intense solitude, she burst out of her human form and let her animal take control as it tried to outrace a reality that felt like a mortal wound.

Finally, exhaustion helped quench the instincts raging through her body, allowing rational thought to surface again.

Get yourself under control, fool, she told herself. He's not dead. Where there's life, there's hope. You can get him back. You *will* get him back.

She stumbled to a halt at the edge of an empty, moonlit clearing, head hung low and sides heaving.

This wasn't the lowest part of her life. She'd been desperate and overcome with despair more than once. But this ranked pretty far down there, and if she wasn't quite as despairing as she had been at other difficult times, the terror of the present moment more than made up for it.

Multiple voices sounded nearby, their clarion tones sculpted by a foreign language.

Panic slammed her. *Nobody had ever discovered her in her Wyr form before.* Startled into rearing, she looked around wildly for the threat. All her life she had been so careful. She could have sworn she'd been careful this time, but she must have miscalculated badly.

The clearing was no longer empty. A strange creature stood several yards away. It stood as tall as Dragos but was far more slender, and it was so radiant that Pia had to squint to look at it. It was winged—not just with two wings but with many that swirled around its figure like white, undulating flames—and its eyes were piercing with unearthly radiance.

All the sick horror from the day fell away, to be replaced with wonder. Even though she had never seen a creature like this with such clarity before, she recognized it immediately.

It had to be one of the creatures that had been haunting the settlement, nicknamed the unseen. No longer barely perceived or translucent, this one was fully present and as grounded in the clearing as she was. Was it really a seraph, one of the mythical creatures that Bel had described from Elven lore?

Her fight or flight imperative tried to take control again. Nobody but Dragos, Liam and Niall, and the gryphons had ever seen her in her Wyr form. There were others who knew what kind of creature she was, far too many others for keeping such a dangerous secret safe, and she knew that sometimes that fact kept Dragos up at night.

But nobody else had actually *seen* her.

Despite her impulse to bolt from the clearing, the creature's noble, inhuman face seemed so… what was the word? Not gentle. It seemed too stern to be gentle. But it did seem, somehow, to be kind, and Pia's panic couldn't quite take hold.

It spoke, and multiple voices sounded clear like deep bells rung from a high mountain. While she couldn't understand the language, all the voices said the same thing.

It walked toward her, sweeping its many wings back and holding out empty hands as if in offering or in supplication. Even though its posture was non-aggressive, she took a wary step back. It looked like it might want to….

To *pet* her?

Umm, that would be a hard pass. She was no tame pet to meekly succumb to a stranger's ministrations. With a snort, Pia lowered her horn in warning. The creature approached more slowly and softened its speech. How could so many voices come from a single throat? She stamped the ground and retreated further.

It stopped advancing. Then several shining arcs dropped to the ground like meteorites, and more of the radiant creatures landed in the clearing. Suddenly there were too many for Pia to confront while feeling so exposed in her Wyr form.

She tore into her human form at top speed. As she solidified from the shapeshift, she opened her mouth to ask the creatures if, by any odd chance, they understood American English, but when her human gaze cleared, she stood alone in an empty, moonlit clearing.

Spinning, she checked every direction, but the shining creatures had vanished.

Why would they disappear when they had just arrived? Glancing at the clear night sky, she walked cautiously over to where the first creature had last stood. Something invisible brushed along her arm, and she flung out both hands as she leaped back.

Was it still here? If so, why couldn't she see it like she had before?

"Who are you, and what do you want—and why did you disappear?" she asked. "Can you hear me? Do you understand what I'm saying?"

She heard nothing but the whispering of wind in the trees.

The whispering...

She strained to listen harder. Was that whispering far-off multiple voices, calling out in a foreign language?

The moonlit clearing darkened. She looked up.

The shape of a massive dragon blotted out the moon's pale glow. Relief and joy rushed up her body, as if she had been a darkened candle and fire had set her alight.

"*Dragos!*" she screamed, jumping and waving. "Down here!"

Dragos's eyesight was so keen he could spot a mouse from high in the air, but he had to be looking for it. She wasn't sure how that would translate to the intense shadows in a woodland scene at night. How could she catch his attention?

Dragos! She shouted telepathically.

Silence.

Sharp edges cut at her thinking. Why couldn't he hear her and respond?

Was that even Dragos?

Even as she realized it couldn't be Dragos—her first reaction had been based solely on adrenaline-fueled hope and not reality—the dragon tilted into a wide turn. As his giant wings drove down, moonlight gleamed on massive white wings.

Disappointment hammered down, even as a certain kind of relief welled.

Not Dragos, then, but Liam.

She rubbed her face and fell back to the sickened wondering if this latest catastrophe would really be the end of them. But this colossal, deadly creature was her firstborn boy, and she couldn't help but be glad that Liam was no longer around to witness whatever the sentinels were doing to his father's body.

As she struggled with conflicting emotions, the white dragon floated low over the trees, dropped with precision into the clearing a safe distance away, and shapeshifted into a human male who raced over to her.

Liam had inherited Dragos's dragon form and tall, powerful build, along with Pia's blond hair, blue eyes, and smoother, more graceful features. The result was a strikingly handsome young man. His shadowed features were sharp with concern. "Mom!"

She rushed to meet him. His hands came down on her shoulders, and she threw her arms around his neck. "I'm all right." The lie was so outrageous she discovered she could say it quite calmly. "It's okay."

He hugged her tight. "I didn't know what to think when Eva said you ran off."

"I wasn't in control of my Wyr side. I had to leave before I did something stupid." His clean, familiar scent hit every mom button in her body, flooding her with feel-good chemicals. Despite herself, she relaxed a bit and leaned back to take a good look at him. Stress and worry etched his features and made him look harder, older. "How are things going back there?"

He shook his head. "I don't know. Once we got… *him*… subdued, Graydon and Rune made me step away."

That made her feel a little better about leaving so abruptly. "He's your dad. That's what they should have done. It's what I would have done if I'd been more in control of myself and able to hang around."

His well-shaped mouth acquired a stubborn line she knew very well. "If I have any hope of leading a demesne successfully, I need to be involved with the tough decisions and difficult scenarios. But Rune said this wasn't the time to push it."

Was that regret or relief? His expression was too complex to decipher, and with a small pang she realized the simplicity from Liam's childhood was gone.

She forced herself to concentrate on the present. "It's going to be hard enough for them to do what they have to do without having to worry about how you're handling it. They're close to him too."

His arms tightened around her. "I know. That's why it didn't feel right to walk away. They should have the support of someone at their back. But right now nothing feels right, so I did as Rune asked and stepped away." His shadowed blue gaze focused on her. "What can I do for you?"

She lifted one shoulder while she did an internal check on the streaks of panic that had been running for hours like wildfire along the edges of her mind. Yep, they were still there.

But running away wasn't going to help evict the entity that had possessed Dragos, and they had no guarantee that—that... (say the damn word, even if it's only in your mind)... *torture* would force the entity to reveal any of its secrets or relinquish its hold on him.

"I need to go back," she said. "I wasn't in control before, but running away isn't going to free Dragos or fix anything." After an adrenaline-fueled day, her thinking felt frustrating and sluggish. She forced herself to concentrate point by point. "Niall's okay. All the children are in a safe place. I don't know where they were taken, and that bothers me. I can't picture where he is or who's looking after him. But none of that is rational."

"Let's find out when we return," he said. "I would also feel better if we knew where the little stinker was."

She squeezed his hand as she bit her lip. "Hard as this is, I have to say no. I can't stand back and let other people fight for Dragos's life. Can you?"

Fire flashed in his gaze. For a moment he looked intensely dragony, hard and ruthless and entirely predatory. "No."

"Right." She gave him a grim nod. "But that decision comes with risk. If that thing in Dragos manages to break the restraints we've placed on it, one way it could hurt us badly is if it found out how to go after our children."

It was his turn to study her. It felt odd to have her son give her such a candid assessment. Not that long ago, he had been prone to chewing through his diapers when he turned into his dragon form.

But she lifted her chin and accepted his scrutiny. She had just seriously slid off the rails, and she wasn't entirely certain she had made it wholly back onto the track. Maybe having somebody scrutinize her decisions and behavior wasn't such a bad idea.

He heaved a sigh. "I don't like it, but I agree."

"So we go back. We find out if the sentinels have made any progress, and if they haven't...." Her voice trailed away as she remembered the terrible sound Dragos had made.

Liam's hands found their way to her shoulders again. He replied in a very steady voice, "We have to assume they haven't. Mom, it hasn't been very long."

"I know. We should assume they haven't gotten anywhere yet." Her own voice shook. Goddammit, Giovanni, pull yourself together. Don't fall apart in front of your own son. More strongly, she said, "We need to get a team together and go back into that hellhole to see what we can find out."

He frowned. "You mean the one you and dad went into when the sinkholes appeared, under the construction site for the music hall?"

"Yes. That's where Dragos got—hell, Liam, this sounds like something out of *The Exorcist*, but I don't know what else to call it. That's where he was possessed." Her eyes narrowed as she thought back. "I think there might be something in that space our intruder didn't want anybody to find. He made a point of posting a guard around the hole to keep people out. It was the first thing he did when he came out of the hole."

His attention sharpened. "What did he say, exactly?"

She tried to summon up the exact words but drew a blank. "I don't remember. I was too busy reeling with shock and trying to figure out what to do. But I remember he didn't want anybody going down there.

Our intruder is not a philanthropic guy. He made it sound like the site isn't safe—which of course it isn't—but I don't think he would give a damn if anybody fell down the hole and got themselves killed. If we're going to defeat him, we need to find out why he wanted to keep people away and to learn everything else we can about him, and that means taking a team of our best magic users down to inspect the scene."

"Okay," Liam said. "We've got a plan. It'll be good to have something useful to do."

Taking her hand, he led her back to the middle of the field and shapeshifted. Despite the severity of the situation, she paused to look at him. He was every bit as massive as his father, just as dangerous, and outrageously beautiful. As he lowered his head, she leaned her forehead against the dragon's cheek affectionately.

"I remember when you fit into a car seat in your dragon form."

He exhaled a quiet laugh. "I remember too."

Of course he did. He remembered everything. "Just look at you now. How do you like it?"

He mantled his wings. "I feel better now that I'm bigger. I'll be forever grateful for the awesome childhood memories that you and Dad gave me, but there was always something inside me that was reaching for more. I think it was my dragon needing to unfurl."

"Maybe so." She stroked his muzzle. "I'm glad it's better now. I don't care where you go, who you're with, or what you decide to do. Work at Starbucks if you want.

Backpack across Europe or tend bar for a couple of decades. All I ever want is for you to be happy."

"I know," he said, his voice gentle.

Fiercely, she locked onto the simple goodness of that moment, drawing hard on it as fuel to face the upcoming challenges. Then she climbed onto his back to settle in the spot where the base of his neck met his shoulders, and he launched into the air.

As he followed the coastline, the dark water and white-capped waves glinted in the moonlight. The heat of the day had eased, and the balmy air felt refreshing.

Mentally, part of her had already climbed back into the hole where she had lost her husband. A part of her had never really left, constantly reliving the stunning moment when he had succumbed to an invisible enemy.

That wasn't what Dragos did. He vanquished enemies. He didn't succumb.

He was one of the most ancient and accomplished magic users she knew, and something had felled him like a tree. A shudder ran through her.

Maybe they didn't have enough magic users to contend with whatever was lurking in that hole. Maybe they didn't have anybody strong enough.

Or, maybe they didn't have someone with the right kind of magic.

In a recent conversation with Bel, Graydon, Niniane, and Tiago, they had talked about the unseen that had wreaked havoc on the new settlement, and the possible reasons for why Pia could either glimpse, or at least sense them, when Dragos and many other people couldn't.

Just as each of the Wyr had different attributes and characteristics according to their individual personalities and animal forms, humankind and the rest of the Elder Races had their own strengths and weaknesses, and they had different strains of magic.

And she was in a fight to get her mate back. This was too important to ignore such a basic fact.

She ran down a mental list of their assets. They had Grace as the Oracle, and Grace's partner Khalil was a Powerful, experienced, second-generation Djinn. He might be able to sense critical things about their entity who was bodiless.

They also had Bel's Elven magic, and Carling was a very old witch from her human roots as well as an elder Vampyre. If Pia remembered correctly, the heritage of her magic was from ancient Egypt. Plus, they had the Wyr sentinels who were all formidable warriors and accomplished magic users in their own right.

There were other magic users in the various encampments in the settlement, in the representatives of Elder Races from other demesnes, but they each had their own agenda and motives. This list was made up of friends and they were the only ones she trusted.

She thought of someone else. Telepathically, she asked Liam, *Do you remember the sorcerer Dragos gave asylum to—the werewolf who settled in New York with that musician and a pack of other werewolves?*

Morgan le Fae, Liam replied instantly. *How could I forget? He's one of the most famous sorcerers in history. You make note of someone like that when they move into your neighborhood. Didn't they decide to stay in New York, instead of relocating here to Rhyacia with you guys?*

That's right. She patted his hide.

Then they're going to owe me fealty when I take over the Wyr demesne. His mental voice sounded both bland and satisfied at once.

Surprise jolted her. *Is that what you've decided to do?*

I'm not claiming it yet. I'm going to finish my time at college like we all agreed, but that's my intention. Mom, that position was tailor made for me. He paused. *Are you surprised?*

Not really. I'm just surprised you've admitted it so soon. She took a deep breath. *When we get back, I want you to bring Morgan as quickly as possible. He has a different kind of magical expertise than anybody else here. I don't know if we're going to need his help, but I want every asset available in case we do.*

I'll bring him as fast as I can, he promised. *If Khalil will agree to help provide Djinn transportation, we should be very quick.*

Good, she said absently, having already moved on to other considerations.

Liam's task would kill two birds with one stone. Not only would it bring Morgan to Rhyacia, but it would get Liam out of the way for a brief, critical time.

Because Pia had a feeling he wouldn't like what she was going to do next, and he would try everything he could to stop her from doing it.

Well, frankly, nobody was going to like it, and everybody would try to stop her. Liam, though, was the one who might achieve it. The others would argue and be extremely unhappy, but she knew they would go along with whatever she demanded.

She was going to see Dragos again. She needed to see for herself what kind of damage they'd done to his body, especially since she was the one who had ordered it done, even if that meant she had to confront the alien bastard looking out of Dragos's stolen eyes.

This was going to one of the suckiest things she'd ever done in her life. She would rather go through childbirth pain again. She would rather be shot—and since she'd been shot before, she knew what she was talking about.

Because whatever they had done to Dragos's body, she hoped they had made it hurt really bad.

Chapter Two

WHEN DRAGOS WOKE he lay in a small forest clearing.

The scene was profoundly quiet, broken only by the distant rustle of wind playing through the tops of trees, along with the occasional warble of birdsong. The sunlight shining through tree branches dappled soft green grass, and the air felt heavy and hot like a summer afternoon.

It felt good to sprawl at his leisure, ankles crossed, and hands locked behind his head as he contemplated the patches of cloudless sky overhead. He could lie there all day, with no agenda and no need to do anything. He wasn't hungry and felt no need to hunt. There weren't any enemies he had to fight, nobody he wished to see or speak to…

(But that felt fundamentally wrong. His bones were very old. They had solidified when the earth was formed, and they knew better. Something deep within stirred and began to push back the overwhelming urge to sleep. There was someone he badly needed to see. He could almost picture her beautiful face…)

But in fact, there was nothing urgent for him to do but nap. The forest clearing, the wind and birds, and the picturesque sky would all be there to enjoy when he woke up. He had all the time in the world.

(But the sky, the sky, the sky was so much more than a pretty scene to contemplate. Like the someone he couldn't quite remember but needed to see, the sky was somehow elemental to his existence.

The sky meant freedom and storms, fierce sunlight warming his wings. The entire limitless expanse of sky was his true domain.

Wings, he told himself. Don't forget you have wings. Your life is so much more than this tiny, petty place. No matter what smaller creatures may call you, you are the emperor of the sky. And you have someone you need to see.

He threw off the somnolence that weighed down his human limbs, climbed to his feet, and...)

He woke up.

And lay in a small forest clearing.

The scene was profoundly quiet, with only the distant rustle of wind playing through the tops of trees, along with the occasional warble of birdsong. The sunlight shining through tree branches dappled the soft green grass, and the air was heavy and hot like....

(Hold on. You've thought these things before. Wait and watch, and you'll recognize what comes next.)

...a summer afternoon.

It felt good to sprawl at his leisure, ankles crossed,

and hands locked behind his head as he contemplated the patches of cloudless sky overhead. He could lie there all day, with no agenda and no need to do anything at all. He wasn't hungry and felt no need to hunt. There weren't any enemies he had to fight, nobody he had to see or speak to…

(There's your lie. There's someone missing. You can't *feel* her, that light, feminine presence that is so fundamental to your life, and you should be able to. You made promises to each other. It is so much more than love that you share, although you share love too.

That's a truth that runs deeper than anything in this scene.)

He woke.

(And every thought that ran through his head was a lie.

He couldn't feel Pia. *That* was the truth beyond which nothing else mattered…)

When he woke next, he remembered everything and knew he was trapped in a spell.

Don't tense up, he told himself. That was what triggered the imperative to sleep.

Relaxing, he let the narrative run through his mind while he contemplated the details of everything around him. Individual blades of grass pressed into his skin. He could see the colorful wings of a bird flitting from tree to tree, feel the somnolent heat of the summerlike day.

But his presence was so ancient and vast that it did not quite fit into the small, inadequate narrative that someone else's magic fed him, and for some reason he could not access his Wyr form.

The spell was very well done. If he had, in fact, been human, perhaps it would have worked more completely. He could see how it might be possible to drift forever, content to sleep the rest of his life away. The sleep imperative would keep the prisoner compliant.

His brain, however, was too capacious to be captured this way for long. And whoever had cast the spell hadn't taken into account the dual nature of the Wyr or the extraordinary depth of the mating bond. You might take away the conscious awareness of that bond, but the Wyr would still *know* in the most essential part of them that something was deeply, desperately wrong.

Stretching, he rolled over and climbed to his feet. He kept his movements slow and casual, the surface of his mind easy and relaxed, letting the spell narrative flow.

(…In fact, there was nothing urgent for him to do but nap. The forest scene, wind and birds, and picturesque sky would all be there to enjoy when he woke up. He had all the time in the world….

Sleep. Sleep. The only thing he needed to do was sleep.)

I can sleep in a moment, he let himself think, feeding it into the narrative. After I get a drink.

(He needed nothing. He wasn't hungry. He wasn't thirsty. He wasn't lonely. He could relax into a deep, refreshing sleep. Sleep. Sleep.)

In a moment.

(Sleep.)

Keeping his movements gentle, he continued to misdirect the spell, not by fighting it directly, but by deflecting the imperative. If he fought, it would probably knock him out again. But as long as he kept his surface thoughts focused on sleeping "soon" or "in a moment" the imperative didn't trigger.

In the deepest part of his consciousness, while he had studied everything around him the dragon had also taken stock of the scene. He realized the forest neither looked like the Other land of Rhyacia, where he, Pia, and twenty thousand other souls had come to settle, nor did it look like Earth.

It was too generic.

It didn't exist.

The spell wasn't just a narrative to keep him snared in sleep. It encompassed everything around him.

Whirling, he grabbed a sharp stick and stabbed himself in the hand. The stick passed painlessly through his palm. He had a brief, lightning bolt realization.

It wasn't just that the scene itself was an illusion. Or that the spell was inadequate to hold the consciousness of an ancient Wyr.

His body was part of the illusion.

Darkness struck like a rattlesnake.

He came awake raging and threw the full force of his fury at the spell, and the details of his cage dimmed.

And there she was, his beautiful mate, staring pointblank into his face. She looked entirely unlike her usual mild, good-natured self. Her face was ruthless, her jewellike eyes glittering with hate.

Holy hells, she looked hot.

"If my husband is dead," she said, "then I have nothing to lose, do I?"

Dragos heard himself start to laugh. Shock and realization struck again. *THAT IS NOT ME.* Outrage surged, and he fought for control—then he felt himself convulse.

Everything became crystal clear. It was night, lit by the cool light of the moon and the pagan gold of nearby bonfires. He was fully grounded in his body, and he lay on trampled sand on the beach. Behind Pia's shoulder, all his former sentinels stood in the ring, watching with cold, wary expressions.

He tried to move and discovered he had been bound in chains. He reached for his Power, but he couldn't access it. Reached for his dragon form, but he couldn't shapeshift either.

Lightning fast, he remembered almost everything. They had spent months planning their move from Earth to the Other land of Rhyacia that held a vast stretch of what Dragos had thought was unoccupied land.

But something had lived here once. A massive network of ruins lay under the new settlement that hugged the shore of the gigantic lake. He and Pia had been inspecting the ruins, had found a sarcophagus, and then *something* had poured into his body like black ink into a well, and he had flung himself into a shapeshift to try to drive it out.

He had been trapped in a bubble of illusion while that thing had taken over his body, and it was blazingly clear that an unknown amount of time had passed. Pia wore makeup and different clothes. She had fixed her hair. The sentinels had had time to travel from earth and arrive in Rhyacia.

How much time had passed? Hours? *Days?*

He caught a glimpse of another personality, existing alongside him like a shadowy snake.

And, thank all the gods, Pia knew.

Dragos had just enough time to snarl telepathically, *Do what you need to do.*

Unconsciousness roared at him with the force of a freight train, and darkness enveloped him once again.

The next time Dragos came awake, he found himself sitting by a forest pool and staring into the calm, glass-like water. His reflection stared back. Dispassionately, he studied the brutal features, the shock of black silken hair, the ruthless mouth.

Some people would call his conscience inadequate. Some thought he was an abomination.

Here is your adversary. This is the man you need to fight. He has stolen everything you valued about your life.

Kill him now.

Reaching out, he touched the surface of the water and watched the visage of the man disappear in ripples that flowed outward to the edge of the pond. Lifting his hand and clenching it into a fist, he waited until the ripples subsided. Then he looked into his own hard, glittering gaze again.

The game had changed, and he recognized this one right away. This was a mirror spell. He was supposed to fight himself until he committed suicide.

But now Dragos remembered everything. He knew who he was—Wyr and dragon, the Great Beast, ruler of demesnes, and Pia's only mate forever. Something foreign inhabited his body and wanted his inconvenient consciousness out of the way for good.

He thought of the time lag. Had that *thing* touched Pia? Dared to make love to her? If he had thought he felt rage before, it was nothing compared to the tsunami of towering fury that washed over him then.

"I've got your number now, you son of a bitch," he whispered, deep in the privacy of his feral dragon brain. "And I'm going to crush every miniscule part of you."

That was a stone cold fact. Now it was only a matter of time.

He fed the spell what it wanted. Soon, he would go after the hard-eyed male staring back at him in the reflection in the water. He just had to make a plan of attack first.

Never fighting the spell directly, always deflecting, he turned his real attention to the problem of how to unravel the spell itself.

Possession was a tricky state to maintain. Dragos himself had possessed other creatures briefly before. It was easier to impose one's will on simpler creatures, such as mundane animals, as opposed to those with more developed, sophisticated minds and entrenched personalities.

But possessing simpler creatures meant you also took on their limitations. And the older and more sophisticated the creature, the more difficult possession became, until it was like trying to ride a bucking bronco. Sooner or later, you knew you were going to be thrown off.

Without conceit, he knew that he had to be one of the most difficult rides anyone might try to take on. Even his body worked to throw off the intruder with the convulsions, fighting it like a virus.

Back in the ruins, his invader hadn't known any of that. It hadn't known who Dragos was, or what his capabilities were. It had just struck at what must have been the first likely candidate in thousands of years.

While Dragos placated the spell with surface thoughts, he studied its construction. Like the first sleep spell, it was elegantly crafted. It was larger and stronger than the first one, but it still wasn't expansive enough to engulf Dragos.

And the details of the illusion felt thinner, less believable. The water rippled but it didn't feel wet. There was no wind overhead in the forest's trees, no birds. This one had been hastily constructed.

Either his adversary still didn't understand who or what he was up against, which was a possibility, or he was distracted by what was happening in the physical world—and that was a certainty.

Reaching deep into the part of himself that the spell hadn't captured, he started to whisper his own incantation.

Smoke from the dragon's breath drifted along the forest floor, seeking the tiny, almost imperceptible cracks in the adversary's spell. He could almost see the bubble of illusion flex in an effort to contain it.

But Dragos's expertise spanned the history of earth itself. His magic could be both delicate and comprehensive. Inevitably, some of the smoke slipped out. Like computer malware, it began to corrode the hold his adversary had on his body.

The illusion of the forest thinned. He felt pain throbbing in various parts of his body. When he took a breath, he felt his real lungs expand. And he could feel the invader fight savagely against his assault.

Then a feminine scent reached him. The mating bond snapped back into place. *There she was again.*

She whispered in his ear, "Get out here now."

It brought him roaring to full consciousness.

He shook his head to clear it, opened eyes that felt swollen and crusted, and growled, "I'm here."

The details of this new scene came clear. He was sitting in a sturdy chair and shackled to it with chains. *Hmm, those chains again.*

They seemed disturbingly familiar. Tightening every muscle in his body, he pushed against their confinement, but they didn't budge. If they had been ordinary shackles, he should have been able to break free.

Oh, these were definitely familiar.

Trampled sand lay underneath, and a large canvas tent had been erected around him. Nearby a fire burned in a brazier. He smelled his own sweat and blood.

Nearby, Rune and Graydon stood tense, expressions hardened into cold, professional masks, clearly ready to intervene if necessary. He jerked his chin up at them, and Rune gave him a slight wary nod in acknowledgment. After that, Dragos focused on Pia.

She looked drawn. Fine, almost invisible lines bracketed her gorgeous mouth. How much time had passed since the last time he had surfaced?

He hissed, "Did he touch you?"

She flinched slightly. It was just a twitch at the corners of her eyes, but it made him so psychotic he almost missed her steady reply. "It wasn't anything I couldn't handle."

"*What did he do to you?*" His deep growl made the tent shudder. Out of the corner of his eye, he saw Rune and Graydon tense. He said to them, "Get out."

They hesitated and looked at Pia, who nodded. "It's okay. We know he can't get out of these shackles. Give us some privacy, please."

Rune nodded. "We'll be just outside. Call if you need us."

Dragos waited until the other men stepped out. Deep within, he could feel the other entity fighting for control, but he would be damned if he would relinquish his hold on himself while his mate was here and vulnerable. They had too much to say to each other.

Even though he knew he should focus on the many important things they needed to discuss, only one thing consumed him. He snarled, "What did he do?"

She met the full blast of his rage with steely calm. "It wasn't much—a little tongue in a kiss or two, a little T&A. He did exactly what I allowed him to do. I baited him with honey, and he fell for my trap. Because I knew immediately, Dragos. As soon as he opened his eyes, I knew it wasn't you." Her gaze ran down the length of his body, and her expression darkened. "Oh baby, I've seen you look better."

"It's nothing," he replied impatiently. When she looked as if she would argue with that statement, he said, "Pia, what they're doing is working. Don't let them stop now. His hold has weakened. I'm attacking him from within, and you need to keep up the pressure out here. He can't fight both of us and win. I'm going to take him down. It's only a matter of time."

The first fracture appeared in her composure, and her lips trembled. As she pressed them together and nodded, he softened his voice and murmured, "Come here."

She complied by straddling his lap and wrapping her arms around his neck. Hungry for every sensual detail, he nuzzled her neck and inhaled her scent deeply, while she ran her fingers through his short hair.

"You scared the living daylights out of me," she said between her teeth. "One minute we were walking along having a creepy and yet somewhat enjoyable moment, and the next minute you convulsed and collapsed. I couldn't feel you. Our bond had disappeared. *I thought you were dead.*"

"I'm so sorry you went through that," he murmured. What if he had been the one to watch her collapse? To feel her presence disappear, along with the mating bond? A chill of horror ran underneath his skin, making his muscles quiver. He had never been good at empathy, but she constantly taught him more.

The delicate skin of her neck was exactly what he needed. He pressed his lips to the light pulse beating a rapid rhythm and her arms tightened.

Then she leaned back to examine him. "You really do look like shit."

He shrugged that off. Bruises were bruises. Pain was pain. The most important thing was that it had a purpose. "You look like the best thing I've ever seen. I need to eat you up."

A reluctant smile tugged at the edges of her lips. "What, are you flirting with me here? Now?"

"Here and always, lover. That's a promise." The part of him that inclined to wickedness wanted to urge her to take off her shirt, but if he lost control, he didn't want the adversary to see her unclothed.

Angling his head, he leaned forward to kiss her, but with one hand flattened on his chest she pushed him back. Frowning, she studied his face, his eyes. "Can the invader see or sense what we're saying and doing right now?"

He shook his head. "I'm convinced he can't. We can sometimes sense each other as shadowy presences, but even still we can't really see each other. When he has control of my body, I'm completely blocked from all physical sensation. He had trapped me in a dream. That was what I woke up to. It took me a while to work through that spell and to discover that not only were my surroundings an illusion, but my body wasn't real either. Otherwise, I would have surfaced sooner."

"You're here now. That's all that matters." She closed her eyes and leaned her forehead against his. "We had hoped the null spell shackles would dislodge him."

Irritation roughed his voice. "Aryal was supposed to have destroyed them. I'm going to strangle her."

"You're going to have to get in line. She's been working everybody's last nerve." She spoke absentmindedly as her fingers twisted in his shirt. "You're sure he can't sense us?"

Dragos checked himself carefully. "I don't know how long this is going to last, but for the moment, yes. What is it?"

Digging into her jeans, she pulled out a small pocketknife, opened it, and pressed the tip to the ball of her thumb until it pierced the skin. As a small amount of bright blood welled from the tiny wound, she laid her thumb against a burn on his forearm.

They both watched as the burn mark healed. Bright,

delicate energy traveled over his body, and every one of his wounds healed. She pointed to his arm. "Why does my Power work in spite of the null spell shackles, but your magic doesn't? You can't shapeshift either. And why didn't the shackles knock that interloping asshole out of your body? How are you two doing whatever it is you're doing to each other?"

"Your Power is an attribute, not an active spell. It simply exists, and my body responded by healing," he said thoughtfully. "Shapeshifting is an ability, but it's more like an active spell. It magically alters physical reality."

"I don't get the difference. Those wounds disappearing *is* a magically altered reality." She snapped the knife shut and slipped it back into her pocket.

"One is magically passive. The other is magically active. That's the only difference I can see." He shook his head. "Or maybe you're unique, and nobody else's attributes would work. You're certainly unique in other ways. As far as my fight with my intruder, that's an internal struggle. It isn't magically altering physical reality. Until we have more to go on, that's the theory I'm going to work with. When we get out of this, I want to study these shackles a lot more closely."

He certainly wasn't going to be stupid enough to give them to Aryal again. Fool me once, motherfucker.

She shrugged, clearly irritated by the subject, and put her hands on his cheeks. Framing his face, she looked deeply into his gaze. "You said it was just a matter of time. How long before you expel him?"

Chapter Three

CALCULATION FLASHED IN Dragos's gold eyes. Pia framed his cheeks with her hands and watched the minute changes in his hard expression.

God, she loved his face. He was both handsome and scary at once. The sheer ruthlessness that could take over his hard features had a purity that fascinated her. He was not burdened in the slightest by the many things that consume modern males—self-doubt, misogyny, insecurity, fear of their own vulnerability, the need to soul search about their morality or question their existence.

For all Dragos's irritating qualities (and as much as she adored him, she had to admit he had, shall we say, more than a few), his soul had a purity that she had never found in any other creature. If you were the rare, lucky person who achieved his inner circle, he would protect you to death and beyond.

If you were on the outside, he might deign to tolerate you, but he would keep watch. And if you showed yourself to be unreliable or traitorous in any way, God help you, because he didn't forgive and he never forgot, and he might exercise all the patience in the world, but he would sure as hell find a way to get even.

And he was singularly untroubled by the possibility of going to war. In fact, she would swear he thrived on it. War involved tactics and strategy, a kill or be killed mentality, and sometimes it provided the opportunity to acquire loot or tribute, and on a very elemental level that appealed to the dragon.

More often than not these days, he chose to take the more peaceful route when he could, but she was convinced that was only because he now had a family. Dragos tried to avoid war out of courtesy to her, but if it was unavoidable?

You bet your ass he would relish the hell out of it.

And while Pia was pretty much Dragos's opposite in just about every way, she was also pragmatic enough to acknowledge that sometimes war was unavoidable, as it was now.

"Two days, max, I think," he said after a thoughtful moment. Focusing on her, he added gently, "Maybe sooner, but I can't promise. I know that's not what you want to hear."

Momentarily at a loss for words, she shook her head and pressed her lips to his hard mouth. His lips softened and caressed hers, so she lingered, helpless to pull away, drawing on the comfort of the moment as hard as she had drawn on the hug with Liam.

Here was the magic they created between them: time fell away, danger was inconsequential, and all the tragedies in the world became bearable. As long as she had her mate, she could survive anything.

But even the best of kisses had to end sometime.

As she reluctantly pulled away, she told him in a husky voice, "Two days is a freaking miracle compared to when I thought you were dead."

"I understand." His reply was just as husky. He cleared his throat and looked as if he might say more, but just then the muscles in his big body twitched, and fury clenched his face and body.

"Oh, no, no." She gripped his shoulders with frantic strength as if she would hold him into his body by sheer emotion. "I'm not done talking yet—"

"Get off," he snarled.

She recoiled—he had *never* talked to her in such a vicious tone of voice before—and lost her balance and slid off his lap. As she scrambled to her feet, she stared at him...

...and watched the fury in his gold eyes fade to amber. Dragos's feral viciousness faded as well. Oh, no, baby. No.

"Lady wife," said the thing in Dragos's deep voice. "How delightful to see you again. Our previous conversations were cut far too short."

She slapped the sand off her butt. "Fuck you."

"You were quite right. Your husband's body is very strong. He has stamina. That pleases me so much," he purred. "Do you miss him? Do you miss *this*?"

Even though he was bound so thoroughly he

couldn't gesture, he glanced down at his crotch where an erection strained, and she had never wanted to kill someone as badly as she wanted to kill him. It.

Raising her voice, she said, "Guys. Time to come back."

Rune and Graydon slammed into the tent again so fast it was clear they had been listening in the whole time. The gryphons moved like the predators they were, laser focused on Dragos's bound figure.

Graydon put a hand on Pia's shoulder. Telepathically, he asked, *You okay, cupcake?*

She wished he hadn't done that, because a part of her wanted to wail and fall into Graydon's arms, and she *would not* show any weakness in front of this creature. Steeling her spine, she gave him a curt nod.

"Resume," she ordered. Even though Rune's eyes were as flat and unrevealing as his expression, she ached for what she asked them to do. Technically Rune no longer worked for Dragos. He was only here because Dragos was one of his best friends.

And because there was nothing more dangerous in the world than a dragon gone renegade.

"Still don't feel like talking? You're making a mistake," the thing said to her in Dragos's voice. "You should always parley with the enemy. You never know when the offer might be rescinded."

"You have nothing to say that I'm interested in hearing." She made herself meet his amber gaze coldly, no matter how much it enraged and hurt her. "You don't matter."

"Oh, but I do," the thing replied. "You see, I hold custody of your husband's body, and try as they might, they can't drive me out. And this internal battle he and I have been waging has been most enlightening. I learn more about him with every encounter. I know his weaknesses now."

"Stop listening," Rune told her. "Now, Pia."

At the same time Graydon's hand tightened on her shoulder and he pressed her in the direction of the tent's exit. But even though she knew Rune and Gray were right, she couldn't tear her gaze away from the monstrosity in front of her.

"I'm going to kill him," the thing told her softly. "And the only way you'll be able to find comfort in your husband's arms is if I'm holding you. The only way you'll feel his cock inside you again is—"

Rage swept over her. Tearing herself away from Graydon, she launched herself at the Dragos thing and punched him in the mouth so hard his teeth tore her knuckles and his head whipped back. Straightening, he started to laugh while blood poured from his split lips. She punched him again with the full strength of her torso behind it, and this time his laughter stopped.

"You think what my men are going to do to you is as bad as it gets?" she hissed. "Forget about them. Forget about my husband. I'm the one you've got to worry about. I'm going to destroy you so thoroughly your name will never be rediscovered."

The disgusting caress in his gaze vanished and he glared at her balefully. "You're going to regret this, you stupid whore. I'm going to make your husband wail like an infant before he dies."

Two days. Dragos had promised. But what if he was wrong?

She went more than a little crazy at the thought.

"You're dust in the wind, asshole," she snarled. "You hear me? You're dust and nobody cares."

Graydon snaked an arm around her waist. She pushed at him, but he bodily lifted her away from Dragos and carried her out of the tent.

The cooler air outside washed over her overheated skin, but the raging lunatic that had taken over her body wasn't finished. "Gray, I'm going to murder him if I have to tear open Dragos's body to do it."

"I know you will, sweetheart," he said soothingly. He set her on her feet. "Try to get a grip now."

"Don't soothe me!" she raged. "I'll get a grip when I'm good and ready, goddammit!"

As she turned to charge back into the tent, she caught sight of several people who stood nearby, watching.

Liam stood with Khalil and a man and woman. The woman had a distinctive beauty and famous, familiar features, with pale skin and dark hair. Partly turned away, she studied the lake with a frown. The tall, handsome man beside her employed no such discretion. He regarded Pia with sober sympathy.

The infamous sorcerer Morgan le Fae had arrived, along with his musician partner Sidonie.

But their presence wasn't what brought her back to herself. It was the sight of Liam, standing with his arms crossed as he hugged his torso tightly, that drove a spike into the nutcase she had become.

The return to sanity was like a bucket of icy water hitting her in the face. She felt the blood in her body throb, the pain in her right hand, the desolation of not knowing if Dragos was right about breaking free and making his way back to her.

But there was no other choice than to trust in her mate. Literally none.

Graydon touched her arm tentatively, breaking the tableau. "It's all right," she told him quietly. "I'm pulling it together."

"I'll stay if you need me," he murmured.

"No, that's okay." She gave him a twisted smile. "Rune needs you more. Keep me posted."

"Will do." With a glance at the newcomers, Graydon strode back into the tent.

Pia focused on Liam. First things first. "I'm sorry you saw me lose it like that."

He shook his head. "Are you... what can I do?"

"Darling, you already did it." She strode forward. "Khalil, once again, thank you for everything you've done. I owe you any favor you need, whenever you ask. No expiration date."

The imperious Djinn regarded her with a sparkling,

diamondlike gaze. "Over the time my Grace and I have been together, she has taught me that there's no need for an exchange of favors among family."

That was such a staggeringly generous thing for a Djinn to say, she had to swallow past a thickness in her throat. "That may be so, but you still have all of my gratitude. If there's anything I can ever do for you, I'll do it gladly."

He acknowledged that with a slight bow.

Then she turned to the waiting pair. "Morgan and Sidonie, thank you coming on such short notice."

"Of course," said one of the most infamously dangerous sorcerers in the world in his deep, pleasant voice. "Liam and Khalil filled us in. Would it be all right if I went into the tent for a few moments? I don't know that I can sense or do anything while Dragos is wearing the null spell shackles, but I'd like to check for myself."

"Please do."

She looked at Sidonie, who gave her a small smile. "Magic is Morgan's forte, not mine," the musician said.

"I'll be right back." Morgan strode into the tent.

Pia steeled herself to wait. Hope was painful, and so was not knowing. To give herself something to do, she flipped on the mom switch and concentrated on Liam. "You've been doing a lot of flying. Do you need to eat?"

His tight stance relaxed a bit, and he gave her a look so full of exasperated love, the imperious Djinn standing beside him smiled. "I didn't do much of the flying on this trip," he reminded her. "Khalil did. And I've eaten some sandwiches. I'm okay, Mom. What about you?"

"I'm okay too."

"But when did you last have something to eat?" he pressed. "You've been expending a lot of energy as well."

His persistence made her think back. The last time she had eaten had been breakfast, and that had been ages ago on this day that felt ten thousand years long. No wonder she felt hollow and edgy.

But the last thing she wanted to do was put food in her mouth. "Good point. Do me a favor—please go back to the house and get me a protein shake. Lots of coconut milk, lots of calories."

She could tell by how his stance changed that he was relieved to be given something else to do. "You got it. Anything else?"

"No, I—" She broke off as the tent flap lifted and Morgan stepped outside.

And there was that damn hope again, clogging up her throat and shaking her hands. She wasn't sure if Liam would notice, but she clenched her hands into fists anyway.

"I'm sorry," Morgan said as he strode to them. "Unfortunately, there wasn't anything I could do."

The crushing weight landed on her chest again. She said tightly, "I'm not surprised."

"I'm not either," Morgan said. "But I still had to try."

"Yes. Thank you." She forced herself to take a deep breath. They were all looking at her carefully, as if they expected the crazy woman to reappear.

They weren't wrong to be cautious. The crazy woman wanted badly to come back. The only thing that stopped her was the sane part of Pia who pinned her down.

"We need to make our next move," she told them. "Carling, Beluviel, Grace and Khalil, and Morgan. You guys are my dream team. We have to go down into the ruins to see what we can discover about our invader."

"I'm coming too," Liam said.

"No." The word came out of her faster than conscious thought. When he looked like he might argue, she said more strongly, "I said *no*, Liam. I'm your mother, I'm in charge while Dragos is incapacitated, and I don't have to have a reason. Just no. You're not going down there, not after what happened to your dad. Don't put that on me."

She didn't have to physically touch him to know how he vibrated with the need to reject what she said, but he reined it in and said simply, "Okay. Whatever you need."

"Thank you." Grateful he chose not to push it, she blew out a breath. "Both Carling and Rune, and Bel and Graydon, have to decide if they can let their mates split up for this, or if Rune and Gray need to let the other sentinels take over here." She looked at Morgan and Sidonie. "I suppose you need to decide that too."

"That's already decided," Sidonie replied. "I have no need to join the party and possibly hold everybody back because I don't have anything useful to add."

Briefly, Pia admired her. She wasn't sure she could make that decision if her mate was involved in something that was potentially so dangerous, but werewolves were different from the Wyr. Or maybe Sidonie just had such a staggering confidence in her lover, it superseded everything else.

"Okay," Pia said. "I want everybody to meet me at the house and be ready to go in...." She had to do some mental calculations, because they didn't have cell phones, cars, or other ways to cut down on prep time. Glancing up, she gauged the moon's position in the sky. "Before the moon sets."

Khalil told her, "Carling, Grace, and Bel are already waiting at the house. Before moonset will be plenty of time."

Liam also glanced at the sky. "It'll be dawn in a couple of hours. Would it be better to wait until daylight?"

Frowning, she considered that. "Daylight didn't do me or Dragos any favors when we had been in the ruins and waiting will only waste time we can't afford to lose. We'll go down as soon as we're ready."

Nobody spoke up or poked holes in her plan, so that was that. They headed back to the splendid three-bedroom prefab house that Dragos had constructed solely with her comfort in mind, and that she now hated quite illogically.

It was still a perfectly fine house. It had three spacious bedrooms, a couple of fireplaces, cool ecofriendly technology that worked well in Other lands, granite countertops, soft close drawers, blah blah blah. But they had barely arrived when disaster had struck, and there weren't enough good memories to offset the bad. She wanted to set it on fire.

The thing possessing Dragos had walked his evil cooties through the house. As soon as she had her mate back, she was going to turn on the complaining wife faucet and let that sucker run. They were going to live someplace else. Anyplace else. She didn't care where or in what. A Quonset hut would do. Like she'd said to Liam, she didn't have to have a reason.

Back at the beautiful, doomed house, Grace, Carling, and Beluviel weren't the only ones waiting. Eva and Linwe were there too, along with Aryal, Quentin, Bayne, and Grym.

Pia left them all to update each other and figure out everything they needed to figure out, and probably talk about her while she was gone. She strode into the kitchen pantry, grabbed her breast pump and some empty bottles, and headed for the bedroom.

Eva caught her in the hallway. She bit out, "Not now."

"Pia, what can—" Eva caught sight of what she held in her hands, took in her tense attitude and the overly wet sheen in her gaze, and drew up short. Then Eva pointed at her. "I'm your partner and your bodyguard. I know you told Liam he couldn't go, but don't give me any of the same shit. I'm going down in the ruins with you. Your go bag is packed. I'll be out here waiting with the others."

Eva's sharp, no nonsense attitude was exactly what Pia needed when she needed it the most. "Do you know anything about how the children are doing?" she asked, her voice strangled with the tears she refused to shed.

"Every single one of them is perfect," Eva said. "And they're all being doted on. Niniane and Tiago, and several other badass people I shall not name are with them. Niall is giving everybody hell, and they can't wait to hand him back to you. We've been getting regular complaints. I mean updates."

Closing her eyes, Pia smiled. "That's my baby boy. When I'm done, please get my breast milk to him."

"Of course, honey." Eva gave her a brisk nod. "Go do your business. We'll be ready when you are."

Pia gave her a crooked smile. "God, I love you. Have you had a chance to get laid yet?"

Panic flashed over Eva's bold, beautiful features. "No, and shut your mouth!" she hissed. "Linwe's just in the other room! You know how Elven hearing is!"

"I hear it's pretty good."

"Get out of here!" Eva slapped her on the back. "Shit!"

Wonder of wonders, she actually laughed. Pretended to be normal, just for a few moments. Then she went into the master suite and got on with her business.

Two days, max. Dragos had promised. And at least an hour of that time was already gone. She could withstand almost anything for two days.

And in the meantime, they might find something in the ruins that could help.

Chapter Four

DRAGOS HAD JUST enough time to warn Pia before the adversary's latest spell enveloped him completely.

He slammed into darkness, but this time he didn't lose consciousness. Iron chains whipped around his body, pinning his arms and legs together, and something shoved him hard. He toppled and fell and fell...

He plunged into icy water that closed over his head, and the combined weight of his body and the chains caused him to sink. He couldn't breathe or swim, and his lungs quickly started to ache.

He was trapped, drowning. There was no way out. No way to shout for help. Panic beat at him with black insistent wings.

Dragos took a moment to admire that panic and the comprehensiveness of this spell. The adversary had not been idle while Dragos had been talking to Pia. He'd had time to craft this attack carefully.

This was different from the pretty idyllic clearing or the mirror spell by the water. It was aggressive, deadly, and immaculate.

There were many types of illusion spells. Most of them did not hold up under closer scrutiny. The stronger and more complex the illusion was, the more it tricked the mind into believing it was real.

And if you built an illusion spell that was strong and complete enough, it could convince the mind of just about anything. Combine it with a panic spell, and you could literally cause someone to die because they believed they would die. The mind was a powerful thing.

The adversary was no longer looking to subdue him or encourage him to self-destruct. He was looking to kill.

Murdering the host you were possessing, however you chose to do it, was an extremely risky maneuver, because more often than not the body died along with its native consciousness, and there was always the possibility that the host's death would take the possessor with it.

Either this parasite was highly confident he could maintain control over Dragos's body after Dragos's consciousness died, or he was desperate. Or both.

But as beautifully crafted as this latest illusion was, it still had that fatal shortcoming—it did not encompass Dragos entirely. He knew better, and he didn't believe it. The chains, the lack of air, the dark, frigid water, this version of his body—the only thing that was real was the intricately crafted structure of the spell that created it.

And Dragos remembered very well the time when he existed before earth was formed, when he had no physical body. When he soared through the heavens basking in a sunlight so pure it was a piercing sword of luminous gold. His consciousness knew very well that he did not need a breathing body for him to survive.

But his enemy didn't know that.

After a few lightning-fast calculations, Dragos continued to struggle futilely. He allowed the panic to sink through most of his consciousness. After he judged that he'd had enough time to "drown" he went limp, and his fake body settled on a rocky bed of sand.

Then he waited, inert, drifting in silent darkness, his mind acquiescent. He had never personally driven someone he had possessed to death, so he could only guess at what would happen next.

If he had truly died there would be no consciousness to cage, so the spell that created this version of his body, along with the chains that bound it, would lose its anchor. At that point, theoretically, it should dissipate.

He sensed the adversary's silent, sharp attention. This was a game Dragos had been playing his whole life, a game he loved: two predators sizing each other up, calculating odds, and planning their next moves.

Here I am, you bastard, the dragon thought, deep where the spell could not reach. I'm helpless and unconscious. What are you going to do now?

Slowly the alien presence crept closer. As he did, Dragos relinquished his attachment to the fake body, and both it and the chains dissipated. He let his mind expand, a dragon mantling its wings—and then he struck.

WHEN PIA EXITED the master suite, she was freshly

showered and dressed in sturdy jeans, hiking boots, and a T-shirt. Eva waited just outside her door and raised her eyebrows as she looked down Pia's figure.

"What now?" Pia asked.

"Nothing, I would just feel better if I saw some Kevlar," Eva replied. "A little armor to guard your chest plate, I don't know, something."

"I get it, but there's nothing alive down in that hole." Pia paused. "Nothing that's physical, anyway. The biggest danger to anyone is going to be magical in nature." She handed over the bottles of breast milk. "Please see that this gets off to where it needs to go."

"Jocasta and Ramone will know who to give this to. Be right back. Don't leave without me."

"Of course not."

Pia walked toward the living room, where there was a large party of people deep into a discussion of magical theory. All of them were dressed in sturdy clothes and leather half armor, with backpacks and weapons. She assessed the group.

Rune and Carling—no surprise there. Rune had not been able to let Carling get too far away ever since she and Pia had been kidnapped. Beluviel and Graydon, also no surprise. Grace and Khalil, Morgan and Sidonie, Bayne, and Liam.

At her arrival, everyone stood. Morgan said, "We decided on an even number for the party going down into the ruins. That way we can stay in pairs and keep an eye on each other in case one of us starts to show distress or act strangely. Bayne has agreed to be my partner, with your approval."

Pia regarded the sentinel who gave her a sleepy-looking smile. The three gryphons looked like they could be brothers—they were powerfully built and had varying shades of blond hair and suntanned skin. Rune was the most classically handsome, and Graydon's features were the roughest.

Bayne had a little Gerard Butler action going on, with a strong-boned, weathered face, a firm, sensual mouth, and dimples that made a surprising appearance when he smiled. He ambled rather than walked, and the ringtone on his cell phone was "Staying Alive" by the Bee Gees. Even the wave in his unruly, sun-streaked hair looked relaxed.

He had also been the head of New York's Wyr Division of Violent Crime for many years, and none of the sentinels had achieved their positions by being easygoing or lax, at least not on the job. She liked Bayne so much and wasn't fooled for a moment by his jovial, easy-going attitude.

"I approve," she said, and Bayne's dimples made a fleeting appearance as his smile deepened.

Liam told her, "I'll walk with you, at least to the ruins. But like I promised, I won't go in."

"Good." She turned when the front door opened, and Eva walked in. "If we're all ready, let's go."

Morgan gave Sidonie a lingering kiss and the beautiful musician hugged him tightly. As everyone filed out, Bel touched Pia's hand with a reassuring smile. "I know this is incredibly stressful and scary, but we're going to figure this out."

She took a deep breath and squared her shoulders. "Yes, we will."

This trip to the ruins was far different from the first time when, for convenience's sake, Dragos had shapeshifted into the dragon and had flown with her over the settlement to the construction site of the new concert hall. The early morning sun had been blazing, and she had caught glimpses of the unseen at the edge of her vision, wispy flickers against the bright sunlit sky.

This time, the group strode quickly through the settlement. It was very late at night, and after the events at the beach party when they had tackled Dragos—the interloper in Dragos's body—to the ground, the twenty thousand inhabitants had retreated back to their individual encampments.

Despite the lateness of the hour, people lingered in huddled groups, talking in low voices around campfires, and watched the group warily as they passed, but nobody approached. The celebratory attitude from earlier had vanished, and everyone wore weapons.

Thinking back to the unseen during her brief flight with Dragos, she thought of her strange encounter in the clearing and beckoned Bel over. As the Elven woman fell into step beside her, Pia told her telepathically about what had happened.

One moment I could see them plain as day, and in the next

moment they had vanished, she finished.

The torches positioned periodically along the path made Bel's large eyes brilliant. *Fascinating. And the change happened when you shapeshifted?*

Yes. That first one clearly wanted to touch me, which was not okay, but I don't think he—or she—meant any harm. Pia frowned. *I've been too busy until now to even think about it, let alone try to figure out what it means. What do you think?*

I think it means you're even more extraordinary than I already knew. Bel gave her a warm smile. *Your Wyr form must be closely attuned to the dimension they inhabit. Their realm lies so close to ours. I wonder what else you could see and hear of theirs? What if you could step into their realm altogether? It would be a form of travel entirely different from walking the crossover passageways or the speed of the Djinn in flight.*

She shuddered at the thought. *And what if I couldn't make it back? I could be trapped in some alien place forever. No, thank you.*

As they talked, they drew near the construction site.

Bayne said suddenly, "I smell blood."

The group's reaction was instantaneous. Liam and Eva flanked Pia and faced outward. Khalil dematerialized and surrounded Grace, causing her figure to blur. Graydon pulled Bel to his side and drew his sword.

Carling, Rune, Morgan and Bayne raced forward. As the others approached, they crouched beside a prone figure. Carling straightened immediately. "He's dead. His throat was cut."

"There's another one." Morgan strode over to the

body, some thirty yards away. After kneeling briefly, he said, "Same here. Looks like a knife stab to the jugular. Very neatly done. With the right approach, the victim wouldn't have had time to call out."

"How many guards were left on site?" Bayne asked. He didn't wait for a reply. Instead, he jogged around the large, jagged hole in the ground.

Pia had been in too much shock to take note, but Graydon, who had also been present, said, "Four. There were four."

Eva swore under her breath. She knelt, opened her backpack, and yanked out a black vest. "*Now* do you see why I wanted you to wear some protection?"

Chagrined, Pia obediently shrugged on the Kevlar vest Eva pushed her into. "I did not see this coming."

"Said every dead person on every damn battlefield everywhere," Eva snapped under her breath. "*Throughout history.*"

"Okay, geez, I get it. I'm sorry," Pia muttered as she fastened the vest into place with shaking fingers. "You can stop chewing on my ass any minute now."

Eva caught her hand and squeezed it in reply. "It's only 'cause I care."

Pia twined her fingers through Eva's, returning the pressure. "I know."

Bel and Graydon, and Grace and Khalil, stayed with Pia and Eva while the others fanned out to search the rest of the site. The scene was weirdly macabre, like a graveyard filled with tombs, with piles of construction materials and dirt casting deep shadows, and the wind whispering through the trees.

Or was it the wind? These days, Pia had grown suspicious of that sound. She squinted, trying to look at things out of the corner of her eye to see if she could catch the subtle flicker of movement indicating the presence of the unseen, but it was too dark, and she felt too rattled. She wrapped her arms around her torso, waiting nervously for the professionals to process the scene and report back.

It felt like a long time, but it must have been only a few minutes later when most of the others came back except for Liam, who knelt on one knee at the edge of the hole. "Only three bodies, all with the same cause of death," Bayne said to Graydon. "They must have trusted whoever came up to them, because there aren't any signs of a struggle. That fourth guard has got some 'splaining to do."

Pia couldn't drag her gaze away from her son. He was so close to that black gaping maw. "Liam," she said tightly. "You're working my last nerve."

He held up a hand without looking up. "I hear you, Mom. It's okay. I'm only looking. Do you know if they left ropes going into this hole when they pulled you and Dad out? Because there's one here now."

"I don't think so." Graydon relaxed his hold on Bel and strode over. "There wasn't any reason to leave a rope dangling. Don't touch it without evidence gloves. It'll mess up the scent. Here." Reaching Liam's side, he dug into his pack and brought out some thin gloves.

Together he and Liam pulled up the rope, and Morgan, Bayne, and Rune gathered to inspect it. A few feet away, Carling stood gazing down into the hole. The Vampyre said almost contemplatively, "There's a lot of residual magic down there."

Every instinct Pia had was shrieking. Unfortunately, most of it was contradictory stuff. She. Did. Not. Want. To. Go. Down. There. Again. And yet here she was, determined to do just that.

And she couldn't stand how close Liam still stood to the gaping hole, even though he was surrounded by some of the most competent and dangerous people she'd ever met. Even if *he* was one of the most competent and dangerous people she'd ever met. Man, those mom instincts. They could be exhausting.

Forcing her leaden legs to work, she walked to Liam's side. It might be entirely irrational, but she felt better as soon as she laid her hand on his arm. He patted her fingers absentmindedly. Most of his focus was on the rope and the others.

"There's Pia and Dragos, which is to be expected," Rune said. "And there are traces of many other scents. Also not unusual at a construction site where all the materials were shipped in. But then there's one fresher scent overlaying it all."

"And all of those scents are Wyr," added Morgan. "I think your fourth guard went down there. The question is, did he come back up again?"

"Only way to know is to get down there and find out," Bayne said. "Let's light it up."

Breaking open several glowsticks, Bayne and Graydon tossed them into the hole. Everyone gazed at the uneven floor below strewn with rocks and dirt. A hint of large carved columns edged the cavernous scene that faded to black in the distance.

Nothing happened. There was no sound, no movement. Rune looked at Pia. His lion's gaze picked up the faint glow from the glowsticks and gleamed. "If our fourth guard is still down there, he's either unconscious or dead."

"Or possessed," she said.

"Right," said Morgan briskly. "Only one way to find out."

He took a step forward and dropped into the hole. Pia and the others watched as he landed below with an inhuman grace. As a werewolf, in some ways he was stronger than a Wyr wolf would have been.

"Aw now, you don't get to have all the fun by yourself," Bayne told him. The sentinel leaped to join him.

Khalil offered, "I can transport everyone else down."

"That might not be the best idea," Carling said. "When you Djinn arrive somewhere, you're like a mini tornado. We don't need for your Power to trigger some kind of magical trap. Let's go down with as little disruption as possible, at least until we can gauge whether or not it's safe to do anything else."

"Rune and I can take three or four people each in our gryphon forms," Graydon said. Rune gave him a nod. "If anybody's uncomfortable with that, they can always climb down." Graydon took the length of rope and let it fall down into the hole again.

Pia patted Liam's arm and smiled. He didn't smile back. He said, "I don't like letting you go without me."

"But you will, because you promised," she said.

His mouth tightened. "I will, because I promised. Besides, I think I've figured out my next job." He called down, "Any sign of a body?"

Bayne looked up. "Not yet. I'm thinking he climbed down, did a little graverobbing to go along with his murders, and then climbed back out again. He didn't need the rope any longer, so he didn't bother to recoil it."

Liam looked at the other sentinels. "Let's assume Bayne's right and he made it out again. I've got his scent. I'm going to start tracking him up here."

"Good idea," Rune said. "Report back when you know something."

"Will do."

Rune and Graydon shapeshifted. Each gryphon was massive, roughly the size of an SUV, with the head and wings of an eagle, and the heavily muscled body of a lion. They were so outrageously magnificent that despite everything Pia's spirits lifted.

She turned to Liam. He told her grimly, "Be careful. I've already got one parent I'm worried about."

"You be careful too." Her mouth tightened. She wanted to send half a dozen bodyguards with him, and she couldn't, not when he was so focused on establishing his adulthood and independence. He would never forgive her if she babied him too much in front of the others. Besides, he might not be an accomplished sorcerer like someone as ancient as Carling or Morgan, but as a dragon, in his own way, he was the most Powerful one there. "I'm trying to think of a good reason why a Wyr would betray his fellow guards, kill them, go into the ruins and then disappear, and I'm not coming up with any scenarios that I like. If he was graverobbing like Bayne said, he might be carrying some dangerous artifacts. Don't touch anything with your bare hands."

"I hear that one loud and clear." He took her by the waist and hoisted her onto Graydon's back, behind Bel, and Eva leaped behind her. "I'll check back soon."

"Okay." She touched his cheek.

Then he stepped back. Moving with predatory grace, he glided into the shadows.

She didn't have time to watch Liam's departure and fret. Graydon launched, and Pia plummeted once again into the scene of her worst nightmare.

Chapter Five

D OWN BELOW, EVERYONE fanned out, moving cautiously and keeping close to their partners. The sentinels broke open more glowsticks, scattering them along the floor, until the underground cavern was lit with a sharp, thin illumination.

Pia was surprised at how many details she remembered: the murals carved in stone that towered the height of three men, and the faint, complex mosaic underfoot. Eva kept pace with her, step by step.

Grace, who had been the most silent in the party until now, breathed, "Ooooh, this place."

Khalil stalked by his lover's side. "What do you see, Gracie?"

Grace spun in a slow circle, eyes wide. She was a pretty, young human in her twenties, with tousled, titian-colored hair and a delicate tan to her fair skin, and a limp from an old injury that hadn't received magical healing when it had occurred. As a result, she would always carry the limp.

She was also the Oracle, from a long lineage that dated back to ancient Greece. Once, kings and emperors from all over the ancient world had come as supplicants to the Oracle, offering vast fortunes in gold, jewels, and silver just to gain an audience.

In the modern age, those supplicants had whittled down to a trickle. As Oracle, Grace was forbidden to charge money for her services, and bore the obligation to grant audiences to those who asked. Her family had fallen into difficult times financially... until Grace had discovered she could help heal injured Djinn.

Now, the Djinn as a society showered her with devotion, and she held an almost unimaginable wealth in Djinn favors. Eager and grateful Djinn offered to babysit her niece and nephew, to provide bodyguard services when Khalil needed to make trips away, to go grocery shopping, and to whisk her home into sparkling cleanliness. No task was too great or too small for them to do.

One Djinn-owned company that offered website services built and maintained a website devoted to the Oracle and managed her appointments with scrupulous attention. At a party, Grace had once told Pia laughingly she had no idea what the website said or how much they charged—she wasn't supposed to know, and the whole process was outside her control—but as a result her financial resources had grown by leaps and bounds. It was a very fine thing to be so universally loved by the Djinn.

Grace said, "This place is crowded with unhappy ghosts."

"Are any of them speaking to you?" Bel asked.

The Oracle shook her head. "Not yet. At least, no one is standing out. Many of them are too worn and faded to be very aware of what's going on. Maybe someone will come forward. Right now, I think they're waiting to see what we're going to do."

"I'd like to know that, myself," Eva muttered to Pia.

"This place is very Egyptian," Carling remarked. The Vampyre had walked up to a column and ran her fingers lightly down the carved surface. "It's quite similar to the elaborate mausoleums our people would build for our god-kings. The language is similar too. I can almost, but not quite, read it. If I had a few months, I'm sure I could translate it."

"I'm not sensing any active magic," Morgan told the group. He strolled through the gigantic chamber as casually as though he were walking down the Champs-Elysees in Paris. "But that doesn't mean there's no danger. There could be magical traps."

"If this is anything like my original hometown, likely there *are* magical traps," Carling replied. "They'll be set to protect things of value, like any attendants that may have been poisoned and buried here to look after their master, jars of embalmed organs, and stores of food. For a tomb of this size and grandeur, I would not be surprised if there was a treasure chamber somewhere. This place would hold all the things the deceased would need to have a comfortable afterlife."

"Where's the sarcophagus you and Dragos

discovered?" Morgan asked Pia.

She pointed into the darkness. "Down there."

Nobody was willing to cast a witchlight yet, which called for more glowsticks, and the group naturally coalesced into a tighter formation as they walked the rubble-strewn hall.

"I'm not feeling the narrative we've got so far," Bayne muttered. "Why would Number Four kill his coworkers, climb down here, and then vanish? To become a guard, he had to have undergone a background check. He knew those people he killed. They were likely friends, or at least friendly acquaintances. They would have gone out for beers after their shifts. Then, suddenly, he bugs out and murders them? This doesn't add up to me. We're not seeing the whole picture."

"Maybe, like Pia said, he became possessed too," Rune suggested.

"Maybe." Bayne did not sound convinced. "We know it can happen. But Dragos didn't run into trouble until he and Pia came down here. Number Four would have had to kill the others *before* coming down here. So as a plausible motive for murder, I don't like it."

Pia didn't like it either. She didn't like anything about this return trip to hell. She didn't like saying goodbye to her Peanut—even if he was close to Dragos's height of six foot eight now and the size of a six-seater Cessna jet in his Wyr form. She didn't like letting him hare off into the unknown after some unknown murderer, while her mate remained bound by null spell chains and possessed by the most unholy asshole she'd ever had the misfortune to meet… at least this year.

She couldn't take it any longer and her resolve broke.

"Bayne." She spoke more harshly than she had meant to. As the sentinel spun to give her his full attention, everyone else did too. "I don't like that Liam went off on his own. We all have each other, but he doesn't have anybody with him. Normally, a random guard couldn't possibly be a match for him. Hell, we all know that an army of a thousand guards wouldn't be a match for him—normally—but we don't understand what happened here, or why Number Four did what he did." She met Bayne's sharp gaze. "Maybe I'm being overcautious, but could you go join him, please?"

"I think you should," Morgan said when Bayne glanced at him. "I don't need a partner. As Pia said, we've all got each other, and I feel no need to wander off on my own. Better safe than sorry."

"I'm on it." Bayne nodded to her, loped back to the area below the hole, shapeshifted into his gryphon form and launched out.

I can just hear Liam now, Pia said telepathically to Eva. *'Moooooom!' But I couldn't help myself.*

No, he won't, Eva replied. *That's a child's reaction—that's what Peanut would have done. Liam's smart and sensible, and he'll see the reason why when Bayne catches up with him. Sentinels work together as often as they work alone. You're tying yourself up into knots over nothing, sugar.*

At that, she took the first deep breath she'd taken

since they'd arrived at the construction site. Eva was right, and Pia gave her a grateful look. *How long do you think we've been down here?*

The other woman shrugged. *Maybe fifteen minutes? Liam doesn't have that much of a head start. Bayne'll catch up with him in another fifteen. You'll see.*

Okay.

As the group continued forward, the huge, ornately carved sarcophagus came into view. Sparks of gold glinted in the reflection of the glowsticks, and a pile of rubble and large fallen stones had damaged one end, breaking it open.

Pia's heart began to pound. Part of her was angry at herself. Lately, she was nothing but a bundle of raw nerves and jittery thoughts.

"If Number Four's motive was to steal some treasure, he didn't do a very good job," Rune said dryly. "If I'm not mistaken, there are embedded gems underneath all that dust. He could have pried out the gold and gems and left a rich man."

"What do you think, cupcake?" Graydon asked Pia. "Does everything look the same as when you and Dragos were down here before?"

"Oh, I don't know, Gray. I was busy panicking when Dragos collapsed." She shrugged as she looked around. "Sure, I mean, spooky sarcophagus, creepy whispers on a dry, creepy wind…. Wait." Her gaze sharpened and she strode over to one of the murals. Eva dogged her footsteps so closely she bumped into Pia when she stopped.

"Sorry," Eva muttered.

Pia shrugged that off and pointed at the mural. "The center of this mural has been destroyed. It wasn't like this before. I was fascinated with it. There was this big battle scene—you can still see it at the sides."

The others jogged over to join her. Rune crouched. "Lots of footsteps around here, and they smell like Number Four."

"Pia, describe what was here before," Carling said. "Try to remember every detail. For some reason this was important."

"It was…." Pia's voice died away as she stared at the fresh scars in the mural and struggled to get past the many upsetting events that had happened since then. The stone looked like it had been hacked at with an axe. "Like I said, there was a battle scene. Very epic. Lots of people. There was an army on the ground, and winged creatures flying overhead. One of the ground figures was bigger than the others. Maybe he was Sarcophagus Guy. He wore a gold crown and he stood on top of a hill. I don't know, maybe the crown was painted, or maybe the gold was real…."

The whispers intensified, and the warm, dry air moved, blown by a restless wind.

Bel breathed, "Oh Lord and Lady, there they are again."

"I see them too, just like on the beach," Grace murmured. "They're glorious!"

Pia shrugged impatiently. "I know, I know. The unseen are here."

"Pfft, I don't see anything," Eva muttered.

"Me neither," said Rune.

"They were here the last time too," Pia told the others distractedly. "There was something else in the mural, and it's on the tip of my tongue. I just can't quite get it."

The figure was bigger than the others. The biggest one on the wall….

…and he wore a crown that shone with a dim glint of gold…

…and he was doing something. Something. What the fuck's the matter with you, Giovanni? Pull it together.

Then it came to her, and her shoulders slumped. "I remember now. The guy held a scepter or maybe it was a weapon. Maybe it wasn't that big of a deal."

"This scene was important enough for Number Four to take an axe to it," Graydon reminded her.

"Are you sure, Pia?" Morgan asked. "Could it have been a sword?"

"I guess. Maybe?" She gave the sorcerer a baffled look. "I didn't stop to look at it very closely."

"I'm not sure what they're doing," Bel said. She and Grace had gravitated to one side and stood close to each other. "Do you understand?"

"I think they want to talk to us." Grace turned to Pia. "Actually, I think they want to talk to *you*. One of them is making this hand gesture." Grace cupped her own ears with both hands, and then offered her cupped hands to Pia. "Does this make any sense to you?"

She finally captured Pia's attention, who frowned, puzzled, until she thought of the encounter in the forest. Her gaze darted quickly around the group. Some of the party knew what her Wyr form was—Rune and Graydon, and Bel and Eva—but some of them didn't, and she had no intention of filling the others in.

"One of them tried to touch me earlier this evening," she told them. "I wasn't okay with it, so I backed off. He held his hands like that."

"Maybe he wanted to cover your ears?" Grace lifted a shoulder. "At least that's what it looks like to me, anyway."

Bel met Pia's gaze. "If they want to talk to you, he could be offering a communication spell."

"Don't do it, Pia," Eva said sharply. "Don't let them. First Rule in Magic Club: you don't ever let a strange critter throw an unknown spell on you."

Bel's expression turned wry. "Eva has a point. We don't believe they mean us any harm, but that's not enough reason to undertake such a risk."

"I know a translation spell or two that could be of some use," Morgan offered casually. "But my feelings won't be hurt in the slightest if you decide you don't know me well enough to allow me to cast a spell on you either. Mostly, though, I want to see what's in that sarcophagus."

"You and me both," Carling told him. "Let's take a

look." She glanced at Pia. "If the unseen are still hanging around, you can take a few minutes to decide how you feel about a stranger, or a near stranger, casting a spell on you. Eva and Bel are right—it's no light thing to consider."

Morgan felt like a better bet than letting the unseen do something to her, but... Pia was pretty sure she knew what Dragos would say about it. She just didn't think she should give any weight to his opinion at the moment.

She glanced around uneasily, catching the glimmers at the edge of her vision. "They're still here."

"How well can you see them?" Grace asked eagerly. "They're faint and translucent to me, almost like powerful ghosts."

"It's the same for me," Bel told them.

Pia hesitated but could see no real harm in confessing. "In my human form, I can only catch glimmers of them at the edge of my vision, but I can see and hear them perfectly in my Wyr form."

"*Ahhh*," the Oracle sighed. "So jealous. That must be amazing."

"To be honest, it was pretty unnerving," Pia muttered. "I'm keeping a tight rein on it, but my Wyr form is fairly crazy right now." She bit her thumbnail as she watched Rune, Carling, and Morgan approach the sarcophagus.

Could there be anything in that contraption that could take *all three* of them out? That sounded outlandish, but never in a million years could she have conceived of that terrible moment when Dragos fell to the ground in convulsions.

Others in the group seemed to have had similar concerns. Khalil quietly dematerialized again and enveloped Grace in a protective shroud, and Graydon dew closer to Bel.

Morgan, Rune, and Carling paused at the edge of the sarcophagus. Morgan murmured, "I think it's okay. You?"

"Agreed," Carling replied after a moment. "There's a lot of magical residue, but nothing active."

"Number Four also left his *eau du parfum* here too." Rune pointed. "Especially where the lid and one corner of the sarcophagus got broken. I think that crazy bastard crawled in there."

Working together, the trio lifted and heaved away the broken stone lid. Eva muttered, "That had to have weighed thousands of pounds. A werewolf, a Vampyre, and a gryphon walk into a bar, and what do they get? They get anything they want."

Pia did not want to laugh. *Nothing was funny right now.* A snort escaped her nose. Torn between equal parts dread and fascination, she drew closer to the sarcophagus and the others followed suit.

Morgan broke another glowstick. It lit his handsome features with a macabre slant. "Well, well, well," he said. "Just as I had begun to suspect." He glanced up. "It's safe. You can come closer."

They ringed the sarcophagus, all looking down at the

contents. Inside, there was a golden human-shaped shell, the lid of which had been dislodged. Inside lay a mummy, wrapped in cloth that was gray and frayed with decay. The arms were broken off at the elbows. Pieces of bone and cloth lay strewn around.

"It appears this gentleman was holding something. A scepter perhaps, or a wand." Morgan's gaze met Pia's. "Or maybe a sword. Whatever it was, it's gone now."

Rune grasped the lid and heaved it upright. Eva said dryly in Pia's head, *And that's another several hundred pounds. I think my ovaries just gave a little mouse squeak. I might be in love with someone else, but I'm not dead.*

Stop it! Pia shoved Eva's shoulder. *I do not want to laugh right now.*

Oh, don't you, sweet pea? Eva gave her a look filled with pure, limpid wickedness. *I can go on for days. I still owe you for that exchange back in the hall.*

God, Pia loved that woman. She threaded her arm through Eva's as Rune propped the bottom end of the lid on the edge of the sarcophagus. It was a piece of staggering beauty, studded with dusty gems and lapis lazuli. He wiped off the golden face, and they fell silent as they stared at it.

The face had large eyes set with onyx, a long, lean jaw, high, strong cheekbones, and sensual, thick lips that were quirked into a slight smile. The likeness was so realistic, there were creases in the lean cheeks that bracketed the sinfully luscious mouth. The unsteady illumination from the glowsticks gave the image an uncanny lifelike animation.

The tiny hairs at the back of Pia's neck raised. She knew who she was staring at. She had seen that same, knowledgeable smile on Dragos's stolen face.

"What do you think, guys?" Rune gave the face another swipe.

Graydon cocked his head to one side. "I think he looks a bit ironic."

The whispering in the wind turned into a hiss, and a feral growl broke out of her. "I want it melted into slag and poured into the sea," she snarled, and the alert interest in Morgan's face softened with compassion.

Back in the direction of the sinkhole, a scatter of debris and rocks fell clattering to the floor. Pia and the others spun around. With any luck the newcomers were Liam and Bayne.

A massive, lithe figure dropped from the surface, landing in a crouch on the floor. As he rose to his full height, glowstick light glinted off short black hair.

Pia heard the sharp, indrawn breaths from her companions, and the metallic slide of swords being drawn. Carling and Morgan raised magical Power that shimmered in the air like deadly arrows set to longbows.

Chapter Six

B UT EVEN FROM that distance, even in an instant, Pia knew better. *She knew.*

The man strode toward her, his long legs eating up the distance, gold eyes gleaming.

"It's about damn time!" she screamed at him. She launched.

He was far enough away she had time to build up to her best sprinting speed. Her control over her Wyr form vaporized, and Lord have mercy, she didn't have the sense to slow down. No matter how fast she ran it still wasn't fast enough, and when she was about ten feet from him, she gave up and leaped.

He snatched her out of the air and swung in a circle to break the force of her momentum, and he was still spinning as his hard mouth slammed down onto hers. She latched onto him with everything she had, arms, legs, lips, soul.

It was just too bad. They were going to have to live like this now and go everywhere together, her clinging to him like a limpet.

Bathroom visits would be awkward. Maybe over time

their skins would melt together. They would become the PiaDragos. Or maybe the DragosPia. Part of her knew she was babbling telepathically like an insane idiot.

"I hear you," he whispered against her mouth, hand fisted in her hair, one muscled arm wound around her hips. "I hear everything you're saying. It's okay now. *Shh,* Pia, stop crying."

She had to drag her mouth away to sob raggedly, *"I can't stop, you motherfucker. Don't you ever scare me like that again."*

His face. His face was everything. He looked fierce, and determined, and tender at once. Carrying her over to a large boulder, he perched on the edge. "Then you take all the time you need and let it out." He said over her shoulder, "Give us some space."

The others went somewhere else. She didn't know where, and she didn't care. "I've been just about as crazy as I have ever been, and I've been pretty nuts at times before."

"I know." He stroked her hair and pulled a strand out of her eyes. "I'm so sorry."

"Stop that!" She slapped his shoulder. "Don't you apologize for what that corrupt, thieving, evil, nasty, smarmy, grasping, parasitic, lying son of a bitch did."

"If I could rip him limb to limb, I would," he growled. His eyes glowed brighter than any glowstick, any forge, and the length of his powerful body felt feverishly hot, so much so she started to squirm.

"You're getting too hot to handle," she told him, in

what someone who didn't know her might think was a more or less calmer voice. Then she thrust her face into his and glared at him nose-to-nose. "Don't make me let go. *THAT'S NOT OKAY?*"

He drew in a breath. "No, it is not. Hold on."

As he forced his Power under control and cooled down, she started to notice details. He was bruised and bloody again. "You're a mess. I can't take it. I've got to heal you."

"*PIA, NO,*" he said with such harsh urgency, it brought her up short. He added telepathically, *The others are still nearby.*

Oh. Okay. She sniffled. There was no time like the present to get everything off her chest. Live every moment like it's your only one, right? *I punched you a lot, and the unseen saw my Wyr form. And I'm not proud of this, but I might be a helicopter mom after all.*

What?! he snarled. Outrage flashed over his brutal features.

I know! I tried my best. I wanted to let Liam go off and be an adult, but then I broke down and sent Bayne after him. She plucked at his dirty shirt. *I hope he's not too mad at me—oh, and I also didn't put on Kevlar when Eva wanted me to.*

What are you talking about?

I'm reciting a litany of my sins, she explained.

Forget about that! Those creatures SAW your Wyr form? He glared around, his mouth set in a hard, ruthless line. *I'm going to have to find a way to kill them. All of them. I just have to figure out how to see them first.*

She yanked at his shirt. *I'm not done talking about me yet.*

"Jesus, give me strength," he uttered out loud.

Her mouth dropped open. "You've never said anything like that before. Y-you're not religious. You're especially not Christ—"

Cupping her face, he kissed her, and she forgot what she was saying. Here it was, what she had needed so desperately. Home. He was home. She was home. She kissed him back with all the longing that had been pent up in her terrified soul. Gradually, her Wyr side stopped beating at the inside of her skin to be let out and calmed down, soothed by the presence of her mate.

At last he pulled away just enough to whisper, "Better?"

"*Mmhm.*" She nuzzled him.

"Me too." Stroking her hair, he told her telepathically, *As much as I am struck by the idea of melting together and becoming the PiaDragos—*

Or the DragosPia, she interjected.

—or the DragosPia, he added with a slight smile, *I'm pretty sure you don't really want to sacrifice your alone times in the bath. Ready to be set on your feet?*

She considered that. *Let's negotiate this.*

Oh, I'm not letting go of you, especially not down here. He planted a swift kiss to her forehead. *I'm just putting you on your feet. We have an audience of eight waiting for our attention.*

I don't care what they want. She scowled at a particularly dark bruise discoloring his hard jaw. She had thrown everything she had into her punches. Had she done that?

He gave her a quick, bladelike grin. *I don't either, but we all have things to say to each other.*

Pfft. Another thought occurred to her, and she shook a finger underneath his nose. *Do not—let me repeat this, Dragos—do NOT become intrigued by any treasure down here.*

He narrowed one eye at her skeptically, as if he couldn't comprehend the magnitude of what she had just said. *Generally speaking, treasure is just inanimate stuff, Pia.*

Then why did he like it so much? She knew what he was doing. He was trying to plant a conversational opening that he meant to walk through at a later date.

I don't care. She met his gaze with an implacable stare. He needed to hear how serious she was. *We've discovered some shiny stuff down here, but before you lay eyes on it and get all dragony, you have to know—this is a line in the sand that I need for you to not cross.*

He frowned. *You're that invested?*

You can acquire all the treasure in the world, and I mean aaaaaaallllll of it. You can barter, gamble, cheat at cards, bust open bank deposit boxes and steal it, blackmail for it, go to war with any nation you like to bankrupt them, I don't care. The stuff down here has evil possessor cooties, and you can't have any of it. I'm not...I'm not stable enough to be okay with that. We'll talk about the house later.

His gaze had darkened with speculation and then compassion as she spoke, but at the last bit, his black straight brows pulled into a sharp frown. *The house?*

She scrubbed her lips with the back of one hand, trying instinctively to wipe away ugly memories. *HE was in that house. He did things there. He ate in our kitchen and rummaged through your closet. He showered in our shower.*

He touched me, kissed me, fondled my breast.

Earlier, she'd told Dragos the truth—that bastard had done only what she had allowed him to do, but mostly because there hadn't been enough time for him to get insistent. And the whole time a part of her had been consumed with what she might have to do if he did.

At her words, the rage that rolled off Dragos was almost impossible to face head on. The tremendous musculature of his body locked rigid.

The dragon said in a deep voice that caused the floor to shake, "I will burn that place to the ground."

The tremor ran through the gigantic chamber, causing the stressed stone to ring with a great noise like a sonorous gong. A scattering of dirt and rock sprinkled down. Dear gods, if he wasn't careful, he was going to cause another earthquake and bring the whole place down around them.

"*Shh*—it's okay," she whispered quickly, framing his deadly face with both hands. "I'm okay. Everything is okay now."

When Dragos's killer side came out, he was utterly terrifying. He said between his teeth, "I'm not done talking about me yet."

"I get it, baby, but we have people we care about down here. We don't want to bury them under tons of rock and dirt." She touched his ruthless mouth with unsteady fingers. "Please, you've got to rein it in."

He hissed, the image of his savage expression burning into her retinas. Then with a palpable effort, he closed his eyes and breathed heavily. When he looked at her again, the savagery was still there in his burning gold gaze, but he had pulled it under control—maybe just barely. She wouldn't want him to undergo any more stress at the moment.

She breathed, "I'm asking a lot from you right now. Thank you."

He shook his head, grasped one of her hands, and pressed his lips to her fingers. Then he eased her onto her feet, kept one hand captured in his, and straightened.

The others had sensibly gathered underneath the clear night sky at the opening of the sinkhole while they waited to see if the dragon was going to cause any more damage to the ruins. Dragos strode over to them, pulling Pia along with him. He hadn't been kidding when he said he wasn't going to let go of her.

"Report," he said to Graydon and Rune.

Well versed in the skill of debriefing, they gave him a clear, concise rundown of what had happened. Morgan and Carling added comments at various junctures, and Grace and Bel inserted their own parenthetical observations about the unseen.

Since Pia had been there for the whole thing, she let it wash over her, concentrating instead on the long, hard fingers grasping hers, the solid sense of Dragos's presence. Now that the thread of almost unbearable tension had eased, tiredness hit her in a dizzying wave.

She fought the urge to curl up on the dirty floor.

After listening to the report, he walked with them back to the sarcophagus and looked at the golden image for a long, throbbing moment.

Watching him, she whispered telepathically, *All the treasure in the world can be yours for the taking, except this.*

The muscle at the corner of his tense mouth twitched. *I agree. This piece of hubris will not be allowed to survive.* Finger by finger, he carefully released her hand.

Then, moving so fast he was a blur, he leaped at the sarcophagus and slammed his fist into the mummy's head, shattering it so hard pieces of bone and cloth flew out. Grace and Bel flinched back, but Pia's attention was caught by Rune and Graydon, who stood watching Dragos with approval. The sentinels had always resonated with Dragos's more feral side.

As Dragos straightened and turned back to her, she said, "I approve, but just so you know, I am not letting you touch me again until you wash off that mummy dust."

He grinned. He was beginning to look calmer; at long last, she was beginning to feel calmer. They were making their way back to normal.

"Since this seems a good enough time as any to start asking questions, how did you get free?" Morgan asked.

Dragos leaped down from the edge of the sarcophagus. "I slipped out of his illusions. He set a trap, I set a trap. Once I got a firm grasp on his presence, I started to… burn him with dragonfire."

Morgan's brows quirked together as he listened. The sorcerer looked fascinated but still mystified. "This was a fight while you were both disembodied?"

"Correct."

"While I'm not sure I understand your method, I'm glad it worked."

Pia was no sorcerer, but she thought she had a grasp on what Dragos meant. When the dragon breathed fire, it was not just a physical flame but one filled with Power. She remembered looking into his eyes when he was possessed and *knowing* that it was not Dragos looking out at her. The fire in his spirit had been missing, those hot gold eyes dimmed.

"So he's dead now," Rune pressed. "Right?"

Dragos glanced back at the shattered mummy. "He was already dead. His—presence, soul, whatever you want to call it—couldn't handle the dragonfire, so he fled. From that point, it was a fairly quick matter of convincing Aryal, Grym, and Quentin that I was really me again, so they set me free."

Khalil turned to face Grace. The Djinn said, "Confirm, please."

Grace blinked. "I don't know what you want me to confirm."

"Is he in the spirit realm now?"

"I don't know his name," Grace said. "And since he's been so dangerous, I wouldn't feel comfortable trying to call him anyway. In any case, even if I do, he doesn't have to come if he doesn't want to." She glanced at Dragos. "And since Dragos is able to injure him, I'm pretty sure he won't want to."

Graydon pinched his nose. "So we don't have any concrete proof that the bastard is really gone."

"Nope." Dragos put extra force on the percussion of the P.

Pia's stomach sank. No, no, no. This, she did not want to hear.

"Postulation," Morgan said. He began to stroll in a circle around the group.

The sorcerer looked as calm as ever, intrigued and engaged. He was a towering maestro in his sphere, and for a distant moment Pia imagined how compelling a thing it would be to have his passion entirely focused on one, entirely engaged. Sidonie was a lucky woman.

She said telepathically to Eva, *While I am completely and happily immersed in loving Dragos, my ovaries just made a little mouse squeak too.*

Eva's gaze flashed to hers.

I might be mated, but I'm not dead, Pia added. She brought one shoulder up in a subtle, droll lift, and the surprise in Eva's expression turned to quick laughter.

"You have Number Four, who did a complex and specific thing," said Morgan. "A very targeted thing that was drastically, violently outside his norm. He knew to come down here. He knew to damage what he had damaged. He knew to take what he had taken. How could he have possibly known any of that?"

"There's only one answer." Dragos crossed his arms.

"He was told."

"Right," Morgan replied. "He had to have been informed. And who was the only person who could have known all of that?"

"Me," Dragos growled. "Or who he thought was me."

Morgan slanted an eyebrow at Dragos. "Also correct. Bayne was bothered by Number Four's actions and motives, but they become more transparent if you consider that Dragos—or so Number Four thought— might have given him a clear set of instructions to follow. If Number Four was a good Wyr soldier, he would be highly motivated to follow orders from the Lord of his demesne. While I'm morally concerned by someone so casually killing his coworkers and comrades on someone else's orders, it's the only scenario that fits."

Grim comprehension dawned on Rune, Carling, and Graydon's expressions, while Bel simply looked appalled.

Goose bumps rose on the bare skin of Pia's arms. She rubbed herself briskly. "But when would he have done it, and why? He was busy getting ready for the beach party, and then we trapped him."

Graydon said to her, "Dragos collapsed, and when he came to, you said you knew immediately that it wasn't him. The moment you got to the surface, we started laying plans. What if we weren't the only ones to do so?"

"Consider this," Morgan said to the group. "Our god-king lay here dead but not gone for countless years. Dragos and Pia must have been his first opportunity at freedom in millennia, so he leaped at it. I will tell you this much for free, my new, very charming friends—if I found myself needing to possess Dragos, I would be extremely uneasy about it."

A hard smile notched the corners of Dragos's mouth. "You couldn't do it. Not if I saw you coming."

"I *could* if you didn't see me coming," Morgan told him. "Because that's what happened, isn't it? He's a proficient, skilled magic user. He caught you by surprise and that was his window in. But if that were me, I would be very uneasy for a lot of reasons—your age, strength of will, nature, intelligence, and knowledge of magic. If you were a castle and I had captured you, you would be very difficult territory to keep. And I would know that, because I know magic very well, just like our god-king does. So, I would not assume that I could keep the valuable real estate I had just captured. And I would be laying plans for my fallback position just in case I had to give ground."

"Fuck, fuck me, fuck," Graydon muttered. "And just as we've been learning about him, he's been learning about us."

"Pia described a scene where a figure wielded an object of Power in a battle with otherworldly creatures. That scepter, wand, sword—whatever it is—must be the focal point of our god-king's magic," Morgan said. "The more he worked with it, the more Powerful it would have become. He must have also made it into a soul repository."

"I've heard of those," Carling murmured. "I've even read some of the spells, but I've never fashioned one."

"Me neither," Morgan told her. "Mostly because they're not a healthy thing to do. If and when I die, I want my soul released into the universe to move on to whatever comes after death. Maybe that's reincarnation, or heaven or hell, or maybe it's nothing."

Grace smiled. "It's not nothing, I promise."

He bowed to her. "Whatever it may be, I know for sure that I don't want to be trapped in a receptacle for eternity."

Pia had started to feel more and more ill as the discussion progressed. She bent at the waist, propped her hands on her knees, and groaned, "And Liam went after Number Four—and Bayne went after him."

"I've heard enough." Dragos strode over to the where the rope still dangled from where Graydon had dropped it earlier. He looked over his shoulder at Pia. "Are you coming?"

She leaped at him. "Hell yeah."

Dragos was too big in his Wyr form to shapeshift and fly out without causing major damage to the sinkhole. He urged Pia to climb on and ride piggyback. Once she had a secure hold, he swarmed up the rope. As a werewolf, Morgan had no wings for flight, so he followed suit, and Eva did as well. The others mounted Rune and Graydon in their gryphon forms and flew out.

"We need to organize a search party," Dragos told the others.

Even as he spoke, there was a rush of wings. Not otherworldly wings in some half-sensed dimension, but real wings that beat hot, dusty air into their faces. Squinting, Pia looked up in time to see Bayne and Liam hovering overhead.

Bayne landed with precision nearby. Liam's dragon form was so much bigger, he swung into the cleared area on the other side of the sinkhole and shapeshifted back into his human form, then jogged around to them.

"Thank you, thank you, thank you," Pia whispered to any god who might be listening.

"You're free," Liam said to Dragos.

"I am indeed. It's good to have you back." Dragos hugged him.

Then Liam turned to Pia. She threw her arms around him. "I've been so worried, and I'm so glad to see you. What happened to Number Four?"

Liam shook his head. Bayne said, "We didn't get him. When I caught up with Liam, he was flying along the coastline. The bastard's Wyr, so he knows how to disguise his scent when he needs to." He said to Pia, "I know waiting to hear can be hard, so we came back to update you. This is not a quick or easy hunt."

Dragos said, "Aryal, Quentin, and Grym went back to the house to clean up and wait."

"I'll get them," Graydon offered.

Liam looked at Pia. "I'm hungry."

"Okay, honey," she said. "Go back to the house and get something to eat. There's tons of food. I can't leave your dad."

Liam nodded. He stroked Pia's hair, lingering to finger the ends, and then he strode away.

Chapter Seven

W HEN GRAYDON STARTED to follow, Dragos told
him, "On second thought, let's all go back and
convene there. I want to rinse the mummy dust off and
change into fresh clothes."

"Sounds good," Graydon said.

Pia glanced at the sky that was lightening with
predawn. The interloper had gorged on plenty of food at
the beach party, so Dragos's body had been fueled
recently, but she never did have that smoothie Liam was
going to make.

It had been almost twenty-four hours since she'd
been able to choke down any sustenance, and not only
had she expended a lot of energy, she had also been
pumping breast milk for Niall.

She was starting to feel hollow and lightheaded. As
much as she wanted the interloper destroyed for good,
part of her was relieved at Dragos's decision. She just
needed a few fucking minutes before the next thing
happened.

They followed Liam back, and the house very quickly
became overcrowded with everyone present at the same

time. A few people spilled onto the deck outside the master suite, which made Pia give Dragos a wry scowl, and he returned. It was good to have such a tight-knit community, but it also meant they weren't going to get any alone time soon.

We need that bigger place, he told her telepathically. *Like right now.*

I know. She stroked the long, powerful line of his back. *We need a place so big everybody can have their own space in it, and then they won't even notice when we leave and get our own real place.*

Both hunger and laughter glimmered in his darkened gaze. *I don't want to take too long before resuming the hunt, or I'd pull you into the bathroom and to hell with everybody else.*

Hold that thought for now. We'll pick it again soon. Pushing his arms away so he didn't forget and touch her with the mummy cooties on his hands, she stood on tiptoe and kissed him quickly.

Growling under his breath, he deepened the kiss before pulling back. Frustration hardened his features.

By that point, she was so hungry she was starting to feel faint. "I have to eat."

"Go," he said immediately. "I'll be there in five."

She made her way to the kitchen, where Liam stood at the counter, wolfing down beef sandwiches. Aryal, Quentin, and Grym were there as well, drinking beer and polishing off a huge platter of wings and chicken legs.

Quentin left the food to give her a hug, and she leaned into him gratefully. "The things you and I have seen since getting entangled with this group," she whispered.

His chest moved in a quiet laugh. "Yeah, the things we've seen. Glad you're okay."

"Thank you." She kissed his cheek then stood back and said to all of them. "Thank you for everything."

Aryal nodded, and Grym tilted his beer bottle at her. They would never talk about what they had done, she knew. What happened in the sentinel club stayed in the sentinel club. But that was okay by her. She didn't need the details of what they did to Dragos in that beach tent.

Grabbing juice from the refrigerator, she drank it thirstily straight from the pitcher and as the sugar hit her system, she started to feel better almost at once. Then she gathered up vegan dishes indiscriminately—a platter of snickerdoodle cookies, a bowl of pasta, and another bowl of salad—and set them on the counter.

"Now that Dragos isn't possessed any longer, we should think about going back to New York," Grym said. "As fun as a bug hunt sounds, they don't need us for that."

"I kind of want to stay," Aryal replied. The harpy sucked the meat off a chicken wing. "I like bug hunts. I just have so much to do with that harbor investigation."

Grym muttered, "I have so many reports on my desk, they've acquired intelligence, formed their own civilization, and are in the process of having babies. In fact, their babies are having babies." He smiled at Pia. "Speaking of which, I'm sorry we missed seeing your little nutcase. You must be looking forward to getting him back home."

"Can't come soon enough for me," she said around a mouthful of cookie. Ah, carbohydrates. "Just as soon as we've hunted down that bug and know that it's safe again. All the parents here must be anxious to get their children back from hiding."

"Where are the children again?" Liam asked casually.

Grym shrugged. "Not our department."

Pia frowned down at her half-eaten cookie, then looked at Liam. Was it okay that he asked that? How could it be okay that he asked that? They had just talked about it, when he had found her in the forest clearing. Liam had agreed with the decision to keep the children's whereabouts a secret.

Dread can come in many ways. Sometimes it hit like a lightning bolt. At other times, it took over the body like a slow, creeping rot.

She stared at the long, graceful form of her handsome son, while nausea churned and blood pounded in her veins. This horrible suspicion... this had to be a PTSD reaction, right? Bayne said that he found Liam flying along the coastline. She had seen Liam's dragon form for herself when he landed at the construction site.

The thief of everything wasn't Wyr. He had never accessed Dragos's Wyr capabilities. But like Graydon said, just as they had been learning about him, he had been learning about them.

And that thief might not be Wyr, but Liam's body was.

Heart pounding, she abandoned her food and walked over to lean against the counter beside Liam. "*Mm*," she said, smiling. "Your sandwich smells good. Can I have a bite?"

He offered it to her.

The beef sandwich.

She met his blue, watchful gaze.

He was very quick, she had to give him that. He must have seen the comprehension in her face and realized he had made a misstep. Even as she shrank away and opened her mouth to scream, he snatched her hard against his side, pulling her off her feet.

Tangling his fingers in the hair at the back of her head, he snarled at the others, "Stay back, or I'll snap her neck."

The sentinels had begun to lunge at him. They stopped.

"*This is why I hate surprises and don't want Christmas presents!*" the harpy roared.

Quentin's gaze met Pia's. His eyes were filled with shock and rage. "But he flew."

"I know." She broke into wild struggles, but the interloper had Liam's strength and speed. He yanked her head back cruelly, and she choked and went still.

The house went by in a chaotic blur. It was a short trip from the kitchen to the living room. With her head forced back so far, she could hardly see anything, just snatches at the corners of her eyes.

Exclamations, chairs scraping across wood. Someone—Graydon, she thought—grabbed at Liam's shoulder, but the interloper spun away, slammed back into a wall, pushed off it to charge through the front door, splintering it into pieces.

The impact knocked the breath out of her. Struggling to get air into abused lungs, she tried to wedge one arm between them while she grabbed the wrist of the hand tangled in her hair.

He hissed in her ear, "I swear to all the gods, I will rend you limb from limb in front of your mate if you don't hold still. Just think how happy that would make me. You've been nothing but trouble since we met, you traitorous bitch."

He could do it. He was strong enough he could tear her apart with his bare hands.

Dragos shot out of the house, barefoot and shirtless and dressed in jeans, moving his tremendous body with deadly, powerful speed. She would have called him an unstoppable juggernaut—she had, many times before— but when he laid eyes on them, he jerked to a halt.

The others poured out behind him. She caught a glimpse of Bayne's horror-stricken expression. "Oh my fucking God. But he was in dragon form. He flew."

Then the interloper in Liam's body whirled to face the house, and Dragos, Bayne, and the others disappeared from Pia's line of sight. As the interloper backed up, he began to laugh. "This body is amazing.

Just like yours was, Dragos. Unbelievably strong. The smells, the sights—the *sounds*." He shook Pia like a rag doll. She felt a rib snap and cried out sharply before she could stop herself. "Tell them to stop trying to surround me."

"Stop," Dragos said.

Silence fell over the clearing.

"He's every bit as strong as you are, your son," the interloper said. "But he doesn't yet have your expertise with magic. He doesn't yet know that struggling against the sleep spell makes it stronger. Now, kneel."

The silence grew deadlier, heavily weighted with the promise of violence and death. Pia didn't have to see Dragos to know that he went down on one knee immediately.

"Very good," said the interloper. "The rest of you do the same—excellent. I am your sovereign now. Say it, all of you."

The words echoed through the clearing. Pia heard the lie ringing through their many voices. Everyone who had been present in the house said it....

Except Morgan and Sidonie. They had also been in the house, hanging out with the others in the living room. If they had been present in the clearing, she had no doubt they would have spoken the words along with the others.

Where had they gone? She couldn't look around to doublecheck her theory, but despite everything she smiled.

"Those shackles you used to chain me," the interloper said. "I want them. Get them now."

"We don't have them any longer," Aryal said, and Pia heard the lie in that as well. "Since we didn't need them, we sent them back to New York."

"That is not what I want to hear." The interloper tightened his arm around Pia's ribcage, and another bone snapped. The world went gray. "Get them now."

"Go," Dragos said.

Someone raced out of the clearing. Pia watched the early morning clouds overhead. There was nothing else she could do. Or was there?

The interloper said coldly, "I did not say you could rise."

Telepathically, Dragos asked, *How badly are you hurt?*

Two ribs. Not bad. The broken ribs burned like hot pokers thrust into her side. To take her mind off them, she focused on the sky that writhed with the unseen.

Hang tight, Pia, he said. The gentleness in his telepathic voice was at complete odds with the rage radiating through the clearing like an invisible sun. *I'll get you out of this.*

I know you will, she told him.

"You do realize that if you kill her, there will be nothing holding me back," Dragos said.

"Yes, I do realize," the interloper spat. He backed further away from the house. "That's why I need those shackles. *Keep back!* I might not want to kill her—for now—but I'm going to very much enjoy hurting her.

Every sacrilegious burn and bruise your servants gave to me, I will give to her. She dared to defy me, and I will crush her underneath my heel and rain pestilence down on all of you for disrespecting my holy resting pla—"

"Jesus Christ, shut the fuck up," Pia snapped.

Her Wyr form had been freaking out for a while now, and she let the insanity take hold. Wrapping her legs around his hips, she hooked an arm around his neck, called up feral strength from the base of her spine, and yanked her head free.

Searing pain blazed along her scalp as she left a handful of hair behind in his grip. Snaking her head around, she sank her teeth into his ear. *I'm so sorry, baby boy.*

Liam's blood filled her mouth, and the world went batshit.

Screaming, the interloper tried to pry her head away. She hung on with everything she had, arms, legs, teeth. He got his fingers around her neck and squeezed, cutting off her supply of air.

Then Dragos tackled them. When they hit the ground her broken ribs ground together, and pain washed over her in a towering tsunami.

Darkness came as a relief.

Chapter Eight

D RAGOS HAD ONLY two things on his mind: keep that bastard from fighting with magic and *get his hand off Pia's vulnerable neck.*

With one flattened hand, he chopped with brutal precision at the nerve in Liam's forearm, just below the elbow. The interloper lost his grip on Pia's neck. Simultaneously, Dragos spat out a null spell that washed over Liam's body, and rage flashed in Liam's blue eyes.

How long would the null spell hold?

Not long. A thrown spell was not the same as the one embedded in the shackle. He had moments at best.

Pia's arms and legs loosened, and her body went lax.

No, baby. No, baby. No.

Dragos caught her lolling head in the crook of his elbow, trying to support her spine. It was an impossible task as the interloper flung himself over, and the three of them rolled entangled across the ground.

"As heaven is my witness, I will break her fucking back!" the interloper screamed. He jammed the heel of his hand at Dragos's face.

If he had hit Dragos straight on, it would have driven

Dragos's nose into his brain and killed him. But Dragos was all too familiar with that maneuver and jerked his head aside so that the interloper broke his cheekbone instead.

Every murderous instinct roared at him to punch the interloper in the throat, but this was *Liam's* body. The blow would crush *Liam's* larynx. Holy fuck.

Instead, Dragos went for the arm the interloper still had clenched around Pia's torso. Throwing himself onto his back and swiveling around, he braced his feet and hips against the ground and pulled on Liam's arm, fighting with all his strength to pry the interloper's hold off Pia.

The interloper roared in anguish, twisted, and brought one knee up to smash against the side of Dragos's head. Then the others joined the melee.

Rune plummeted like a meteor on the interloper's legs, pinning them with his torso, and Graydon and Bayne lunged into play too, reaching around Dragos and Pia to grab Liam's arm and lend their strength to prying him loose. Quentin threw himself into the writhing pile, reaching with both hands to shield Pia's head from any blows.

Then Dragos caught a glimpse of Khalil striding toward them, long dark hair blown across his face and partially obscuring his brilliant, diamondlike gaze. Laying one hand on Pia's shoulder, Khalil announced, "I will remove this one now."

The Djinn's Power raised, and a maelstrom washed

over them. When it died, both he and Pia were gone.

Roaring, the interloper bucked and kicked. Liam's body was so strong, he threw Rune and Dragos off. Immediately, Dragos flipped to his feet and began the lunge back into the fight....

He felt it, then. The null spell dissipated, and Liam's human body shimmered and transformed into the dragon whose giant body dominated the scene. Still roaring, the white dragon spun around and swiped at the combatants with immense, deadly talons.

Graydon dropped and rolled. One blow scooped Quentin into the air. He slammed into a tree and plummeted like a stone. Another caught Bayne and scored down his torso. Bayne's blood sprayed Dragos in the face.

There were other sounds, screams and shouts. Other magics. At the far edge of the clearing, Eva, Bel and Carling worked over Pia's prone figure, while Khalil and Grace stood watching at her feet. Eva knelt at Pia's head, cupping it in her hands. He could smell Pia's blood.

Why was there blood?

Dragos threw himself into a shapeshift, and everything around him grew smaller. Fast as a cat, the white dragon whirled to confront him.

The reality slammed Dragos like another body blow.

Not in the entirety of his whole wicked life had he faced an enemy like this. They were the same size. The same in strength.

And this was his son.

The white dragon crouched, wings mantled and tail lashing, and bared long, razor-sharp teeth. He hissed, "If I knew how to breathe fire, they would already be burning. I might not know how to yet, but I vow I will learn."

"You can't win this fight," Dragos said coldly. Inside he was rigid with terror. Telepathically, he roared, *IS SHE ALIVE?*

Bel looked up at him. *Yes.*

YES was a desperately insufficient answer. He needed to know what was wrong and longed to race over there, but he did not dare turn away from the threat facing him.

"This is my land," the white dragon growled. "*My land*, do you hear? I rule this kingdom. Anyone who stays is supplicant to me!"

"You're an infestation," Dragos snarled. Out of the corner of his eye, he saw the other sentinels shapeshift into their Wyr forms until three gryphons, a gargoyle, and a black panther ringed the two dragons. The panther was limping, and one of the gryphons was streaked with blood, but they were all in fighting form. The sentinels kept their focus squarely on the white dragon, watching him with calculating predators' eyes. "You're dead, and your kingdom is dead along with you."

The white dragon narrowed his eyes. "Leave this land and I will let you and the others live," he purred.

"I don't negotiate with terrorists." Dragos paced around the other dragon, in the direction opposite from where Pia and the other women were, and the interloper turned with him.

Come on, Liam. Fight him, son.

"No? Then I look forward to finding your hidden children." The white dragon looked down at himself. "This body has a tremendous appetite. I'm sure their tender little bodies will be indescribably delicious."

Dragos could almost hear what Pia would have said had she been conscious. *Oh my fucking God, he's still talking.* He agreed with her. He'd heard more than enough.

As he lunged forward, the white dragon crouched down even further and launched into the air. Twisting, Dragos reached for the other dragon. His talons raked Liam's hind leg, but he just missed grasping hold of him.

Just then Aryal raced into the clearing. She wore a backpack. Looking around, her expression filled with affront. "I gave you guys as long as I thought I could. What the fuck happened?"

Dragos vibrated with conflicting needs. He needed to chase after the other dragon, but he needed to check on Pia more. "Follow him but don't engage," he said to the other sentinels. "I'll catch up with you."

The black panther leaped onto Bayne's broad back, and the winged Wyr shot into the sky. Aryal spun in a circle, looking frustrated. As long as she held the null spell shackles, she couldn't shapeshift into her Wyr form and join them.

Finally, she dashed over to where Eva crouched and

threw the backpack at her. Eva didn't move her hands from supporting Pia's head, but she jerked her face away. The backpack hit her in the shoulder.

"Guard this," Aryal ordered.

"Ow! Fuck you, you fucking whack job," Eva snapped. "Can you not fucking see I am helping to save someone's fucking life here? I don't take fucking orders from you!"

Not bothering to reply, Aryal shapeshifted into her harpy form and launched after the other sentinels.

During that exchange, Dragos shapeshifted into his human form and raced over to kneel at Pia's shoulder. There was so much blood around her head, Eva's hands were soaked with it. They would have to burn the blood so that there was no trace left of it. He thrust the thought aside.

"What happened? *What happened?*" Carefully, he laid a hand on her chest, over her heart.

Before he could sink his awareness into her body to see for himself, Bel lifted his hand away and with a gentle tug, she pulled his attention away from Pia's pale, still face. He was not sure he would have allowed that from anyone else, but Bel was special to Pia so he focused on the Elven woman's compassionate face.

"While the blood is frightening, it's not important," Bel told him. "When Pia attacked him, he was holding onto a fistful of her hair. She tore her scalp to get free from his hold." She gave him a small, wry smile. "An action like that took a lot of determination, and it had to have been excruciating, but it wasn't life-threatening. The serious injuries are internal. He was crushing her alive. She sustained four broken ribs, a spinal injury, and took some organ damage. Carling is working on healing those now."

That was all he could bear to hear. He pulled away from Bel's hold, stroked the tangled hair back from Pia's face, and sank his awareness into her body. Grimly, he obsessed over every injury, but Bel had been very accurate in her description.

One of her kidneys... He wasn't sure it could be saved, and he wiped his mouth at the sickened feeling in his gut. He was tempted to add his Power to the effort, but he knew better than to intrude on someone else while they were in the middle of a delicate healing.

"When can she wake up?" he asked.

"Dragos," Grace said very gently. The Oracle's pretty face was streaked with tears, her eyes filled with the black of the goddess Nadir's depths. "Her body is alive, but her soul isn't there."

He shook his head sharply. Those words...

They were unimaginable.

"What the fuck are you saying?"

"I'm saying that we have to ask her soul to come back," the Oracle said. "And I don't think it matters if you're religious or not, because I think we have to pray."

The ground around Dragos smoked. He surged to his feet. Then he reached out telepathically further than he'd ever had before. *Azrael.*

I am here, brother. For the first time, Dragos noticed the god of Death standing under the shade of a nearby tree. Nobody else seemed to notice his presence.

Only one person could make Dragos feel this extreme kind of terror. Out of countless kingdoms and nations and epochs, out of an endless panoply of outsized villains and magicians and petty tyrants filled with meanness and greed, only one.

Only one.

And ironically that would be the last thing she would ever want to do, to make him feel this afraid. But it happened every time her life was in danger. Being so desperately in love with someone and mating with them—it came with a heavy price.

And he paid it gladly, and he would keep paying it again and again, but holy gods just let her come back.

Was that a prayer?

He stalked over to Azrael. *Give her back, goddammit. This is my mate. She is my life. Her body is still working. You have got to let her come back.*

I don't have her, Dragos. Death's green gaze was regretful. *She is in another realm now.*

WHEN PIA OPENED her eyes, she lay in the arms of a seraph who knelt at the base of a vast tree. Her wondering gaze traveled from the noble, radiant face bent over hers, to the many wings flowing from its back.

She had no idea what to do with that, so she looked at the trunk of the tree, but it kept going and going, fading into the distance on either side. And she had no idea what to do with *that*, so her gaze traveled upward to the intricate canopy of branches and leaves overhead.

The tree filled the sky as far as the eye could see. It was as big as a mountain, maybe bigger. Countless shining seraphim flew among the branches.

Oh, my lands...

It was too magnificent to look at for long. After staring a few moments, she couldn't bear to take in any more. Averting her gaze, she searched for familiar landmarks in an effort to get some grounding.

In the distance, a graceful figure danced. She or he had long black hair. As she... he? pirouetted, his... her? hair whirled around them, creating and recreating an infinite variety of patterns. The dancer was utterly mesmerizing, indescribably beautiful.

Feeling overwhelmed, tears rolled down Pia's cheeks. Carefully the seraph wiped them away.

"Am I hallucinating?" she asked.

She raised a hand to touch her own cheek. Only then did she realize that she wasn't wearing her cloaking spell, and her skin shone with the delicate, pearlescence of the moon.

"Shining One," the seraph said in its many voices that rang like the deep tolling of a bell. "Welcome to our realm. We are so very pleased to welcome thee here."

The multitude of voices resonated throughout her being, and she felt herself vibrate like a tuning fork. And it wasn't lost on her that she could understand the seraph now. Had it cast a communication spell on her, or was it from the Power of just being in this place?

"Your realm is very beautiful, but I didn't mean to come. This has to be some kind of mistake." She pushed upright, and the seraph eased her into a sitting position against a root of the tree.

"We laugh, we cry, and we learn. There is never a mistake," the seraph told her. "We beseeched our Lord and Lady, and they granted our petition for thou to come."

Thee and thou? Beseeched? She couldn't be hallucinating. Her brain didn't have the capacity to make this up. She felt the back of her head and pressed a hand to her side. She felt no pain, no exhaustion, and no hunger either. In fact, she had never felt better in her life. "Where are your Lord and Lady?"

The seraph gestured to the dancer who soared into a leap that was impossibly thrilling to witness. Pia wiped her face, which had somehow become wet again.

"Okay," she said. "I can see they're busy. When will they stop so I can talk with them about going home?"

The seraph gazed at her. "They do not stop. The Dancer dances the universe into existence. We tend to the Tree and pay homage to the dance. That is our privilege and purpose."

The Dancer dances....

Shakily she asked, "Are you saying *that* is Taliesin?"

To the Elder Races, the seven Primal Powers were the linchpins of the universe. Taliesin, the god of the

Dance, was the first among the Primal Powers because everything dances, the planets and all the stars, other gods, people, molecules, everything. Dance was change, and the universe was constantly in motion.

Then there was Azrael, the god of Death; Inanna, the goddess of Love; Nadir, the goddess of the depths or the Oracle; Will, the god of the Gift; Camael, the goddess of the Hearth; and Hyperion, the god of Law.

The seven gods existed in a pantheon of mythology, but Pia had met Azrael more than once, talked with him, and had slapped his face when she was in labor, and he looked almost exactly like Dragos, who was known throughout the Elder Races as the Great Beast.

Dragos liked to shrug away the whole topic by saying there were any number of extremely Powerful creatures who could do miraculous, magical things, including Pia, and he was right. And honestly, the whole subject made her extremely uncomfortable, so she was just as happy to leave it alone and enjoy living her life.

But this place—this was far beyond anything she had ever experienced or could have imagined. The grass underneath her legs was exceptionally, compellingly green. The light in the seraph's ageless gaze was endlessly absorbing, and she felt like she could gaze into its eyes forever. This realm was so intensely alive and real, it made the rest of her life feel pale and far away.

She didn't want the rest of her life to feel pale and far away. For the most part, she was happier than she had ever dreamed possible. She adored her mate, and she loved her… She loved her children. There was something wrong with one of them, wasn't there? What were their names?

Panic blew out her mind. As she sprang to her feet, the seraph straightened too and faced her. "I need to go back," she said urgently. "This place—it's so incredible, but it's doing something to my mind and just now I couldn't think of my children's names. I still can't. My children—do I have boys or girls? I'm not sure anymore. They are the loves of my life. *That is unacceptable, do you hear me?*"

"We hear and understand," the seraph replied. "For those who visit our realm, sooner or later, they all want to give up their previous existence and stay. We would welcome that from thee if thou wished."

"Thank you, but I do *not* wish to give up my life!"

"Then listen as I tell thee an important tale, because we do not have much time." The seraph took her hands. "Once there was a very Powerful and wicked ruler. His name was Senusret. He wanted things that were not his to take. He summoned one of my brethren to his kingdom—to thy realm—and killed that which should never be killed."

"He killed a seraph?"

It bowed its head in reply, and overhead all the seraphim raised their voices in outcry. That sound… she wanted to fall to her knees under the weight of the tragedy and barely managed to stay upright. "I'm so sorry for your loss."

"Our brethren is cut off from the dance of life," the seraph told her, the lines of its face marked with grief. "Senusret bound its soul to infuse an item with everlasting Power. We cannot conceive of a more terrible fate. We have tried—for millennia we have tried—to find a way to cross the bridge to bring the soul of our brethren home. Then we bore witness as thine people arrived. We knew that Senusret merely slept and if disturbed, his evil would awaken again, and so we tried to gain the attention of thine people and warn thee. But to no avail. Now that he has awakened again, no realm is safe from his insatiable greed."

"Senusret," she said, trying out the strange name. "I've called him the thief of everything."

"Among thine many gifts, thou art a truth teller." The seraph placed its fingers on her brow between her eyes, and the Power from its touch filled her mind with light. "Shining One, we beseech thee—please help to bring the soul of our lost brethren home."

She took the seraph's long, strange hand in both of hers. "I will do my very best for you, but first you must send me back."

Chapter Nine

WHEN SHE NEXT came aware, she heard two voices talking quietly.

"None of us could have predicted this," Death said. "That the dragon, who was terminally possessive and loved the material treasures of the world beyond all else, would come to yearn eternally for what he could never truly hold onto: the soul of another. All things die, brother. Sooner or later, they all die."

"Get out of my fucking face, you morbid bastard." Dragos's voice sounded ragged and very tired.

She became aware of other things. Dragos held her in his lap, her head cradled in the crook of his arm. The sun had risen high enough to turn the morning hot. Being held by him was her absolute favorite thing in the world. She could while away countless hours simply resting against his side.

"I knew she would be your doom," Death said. "I just wish—I wish you hadn't fallen in love."

"Why?" Dragos asked. "You did once."

"Yes, and she died. And I'm not Wyr. In any case, that happened a very long time ago. It's ancient history."

She had never heard Dragos and Azrael talk together like this before, and she was afraid to hear what they might say next. Opening her eyes, she contemplated Dragos's harsh profile. He looked... bleak. Unutterably lonely.

"He's wrong," she said and watched Dragos's expression flare to life. "You can always hold onto me."

His body clenched, but he cradled her as though she were spun glass. There were tears in his eyes. Dragos never cried. "I thought you were gone."

"I'm so sorry." She wrapped an arm around his neck. "I was, but I'm back now."

It's going to take a long time for that to be better, he told her telepathically.

We will have that time and so much more, she whispered.

His mental voice was nearly inaudible. *Swear it.*

I swear it on my life. She kissed his cheek, his chin, his lips. He rested his mouth over hers, inhaling her breath, exhaling his. Sharing life. It was as intimate as anything they had ever shared. Finally, reluctantly, she pulled back and asked aloud, "Where's Liam?"

"He turned into a dragon and flew off. The sentinels are tracking where he goes. I told them I would catch up, but I couldn't leave you yet." He pressed his lips to her forehead.

"Now I can go with you."

He said fiercely, "No. *No way in hell*, Pia. The only place you're going is into a hospital bed under heavy guard."

Taking a piece of his short, silky hair, she wound it around her fingers. "I dissent."

"You almost died! For fuck's sake—your soul left your body!" Rage vibrated through him.

But she knew him very well, and knew that his rage really stemmed from fear. "Yes, well, that was actually intentional." When his head reared back and he stared at her in equal parts fury and incredulity, she lifted one hand quickly. "Not by me! I didn't do it! The seraphim did, because they had things to say. Our thief's name is Senusret. A very long time ago, he summoned and killed one of them, and trapped its soul in his wand thingy to imbue it with the seraph's Power. They want the soul of their seraph back, and I said we would help them. There's more…" She paused, thinking of the tree and the dancer. "Honestly, I'm too overwhelmed to talk about it."

"You tell me everything," he said with quick jealousy. "Every breath you took. Every word you said, everything you thought. You don't get to go that far away from me without repercussions."

He was so fierce, she almost wanted to smile. Almost, except his pain was too recent and still too raw. "I will, I promise. But that's not urgent, and Liam's situation is."

He took her by the shoulders. His hard hands were not quite steady. "You. Almost. Died. There was spinal damage. Organ damage. You ripped your own hair out."

Frowning, she absorbed all that. After a moment, she

said, "Yeah, but I actually feel fine? Shouldn't I be feeling shaky or something?"

"Yes, you should." He narrowed his eyes. "How fine is fine?"

In answer, she rolled off his lap and onto her feet, then executed a little jump into a "ta-da" stance with her hands up. "Fine, apparently."

He rose more slowly, staring at her. "What are you doing?"

"I'm doing jazz hands." She waved her hands at him.

After a tense, unsmiling moment, he said, "Do it again."

"What, this?" She hopped into another "ta-da" position, hands out. "See what I mean? Jazz hands. Dragos, I get that I shouldn't be, but I'm really fine. Like, I could run a marathon fine. Maybe that was a parting gift from the seraphim."

"I'll take it." Grabbing her by the hand, he hauled her into a tight hug.

When he didn't let her go, she shifted a bit. Then wiggled some. "Honey, what are you doing?"

His arms loosened, and with obvious reluctance, he let her go. "Grace said we needed to ask your soul to come back, and then we needed to pray. I'm not any good at either asking or praying, but I did my best. So I thought I should also say thank you."

Oh, her heart. Every time she thought she couldn't love him more, somehow he made it happen. Taking one of his hands, she kissed it.

Then she looked around. Azrael had vanished (no surprise there; it's who he was and what he did). The front of the nearby house she had grown to hate so much was a wreck (yay!). Some of their friends (but none of the sentinels) were gathered on the lawn in front of the house, standing or sitting on the ground and watching them.

Eva stood close to Linwe, wearing a backpack (which looked odd) and holding hands with the young Elven woman. (Oooh, their romance appeared to have progressed!) Even from that distance, Pia could see the tearstains on Eva's face. It made Pia's heart hurt to look at her.

She said softly, "Oh, baby girl."

Eva broke away from Linwe and raced over to her. "I hate you."

It made no sense, but Pia didn't mind. She heard the real message behind the words, and it was one of love and pain. She hugged Eva tight. "I know you do. I deserve it."

"You really do." Eva's voice was thick. "What the fuck was that fight? You tore your hair out—you lost a chunk of your scalp. You *bit* him? I was so fucking proud of you until you almost died. Then I was over it."

"I was too." Thinking about the fight, at least the part she was conscious for, made her shudder. "Why are you wearing a backpack?"

"Because of that psycho harpy," Eva spat. "These are the null spell shackles. I had my hands literally full keeping your bloody skull straight while Carling and Bel worked on you, and we all thought you were going to die, and then Aryal threw these at me and told me to guard them. I'm going to hurt her for that. I'm not asking for permission. I'm telling you what's going to happen."

"That sounds awful. I'm so sorry." She rubbed Eva's arm, frowned, and went telepathic. *How much did I bleed?*

Her blood was too full of magic. They could never afford to leave any of it around, because if it were found by the right curious individual, they would be able to discover what her Wyr form was.

Don't worry about it. I handled it. I burned everything except for what got smeared on your clothes.

While they talked, Pia watched over Eva's shoulder as Morgan and Sidonie walk out of the house. As they drew near, Morgan asked, "Is it acceptable to approach now?"

"Yes," Dragos said. "What is it?"

"First, felicitations on your recovery," Morgan told Pia. "We have been deeply concerned for you."

Beside him, Sidonie gave Pia a slanted smile and mouthed, "Sometimes he's a little old-fashioned."

For a brief moment, the little interlude pulled Pia out of her worry over Liam and she felt completely charmed by the other couple. "Thank you."

"Secondly…" Morgan had a pack over one shoulder too, which he unzipped and opened. "When Sidonie and I realized that our god-king had possessed Liam, we slipped away. You see, Liam hadn't gotten very far before Bayne caught up with him. Not very much time had passed, and it had to have been eventful, because Number Four had disappeared and so had the artifact. I was pretty sure they couldn't have gotten far—and I was right." He pulled out a slender object wrapped in leather, and as he held it out, he unwrapped it, making sure not to touch what was inside. "We found Number Four's body along with the artifact in a cave high on a bluff. He hadn't had the time to do anything more elaborate."

Pia moved close to Dragos as they stared at what Morgan held. It was a scepter (of course it was, because what else would that jerk have used?), and a deep, radiant Power emanated from it. With a pang, she thought of the dead seraph's soul, trapped in it.

"What are you saying?" She frowned. "I don't understand."

"Here's what I think happened," Morgan said. "Our god-king—"

"His name is Senusret," she told him.

"Is it?" Morgan's glance was quick and alert. "Interesting. I'd love to know how you learned that. Anyway, as we'd discussed earlier, Senusret must have laid his contingency plans with Number Four as soon as you were both pulled out of the sinkhole. And then Number Four followed orders. He killed the other guards, retrieved the soul repository, and ran." He turned to Dragos. "Meanwhile you made Senusret so uncomfortable, he finally relinquished his stolen castle and fled. When that happened, the soul repository acted like a magnet and drew him back to it. Probably at that point, he possessed Number Four and took control of the scepter. At least that's what I would have done if I were him. And then Liam showed up."

"And we know the rest from there." Dragos took the scepter, handling it like Morgan had, through the leather. "Thank you, Morgan. Your help has been extraordinary."

"It was truly my pleasure. I know you had misgivings about giving us asylum when we moved to New York. I've been very happy to repay that decision with any help I could."

Peeling back the leather, Dragos studied the gold scepter. Pia waited as long as she could stand it. Then she murmured, "He's taking Liam further away every minute. Can we give this to the seraphim and go after him now?"

Dragos's gold gaze narrowed in thought. "Every time he has possessed someone, they were near this—me, probably Number Four, and then Liam. He needs this as an anchor and to move from body to body, correct?"

"Yes," Morgan said. "Now that he has no living body of his own, the soul repository is critical."

"So if we get rid of the repository, he loses the ability to possess someone else. But what happens if the repository is in another realm? Can it still draw him back into it?"

"I don't know, maybe," Morgan admitted. "For a

soul, distance is very different from what it is to us."

Dragos met Pia's gaze. "If we gave this to them now, Senusret might be able to possess a seraph. And in any case, I'm not willing to let him escape to another realm. I want this fucker gone for good. We have to figure out a way to drive him out of Liam. Maybe he'll leave more willingly if he knows this is close by."

Morgan said carefully, "If you make things uncomfortable enough for him, he could choose to voluntarily leave Liam, like he did with you."

That bad, bad feeling was back in the pit of Pia's stomach. She pressed a hand to her forehead. "Liam's too Powerful, and he loves power too much. The only way he's going to leave my son is if he's forced to."

"So we'll force him."

"But how?"

"We'll find a way." Dragos's features set with ruthless determination. "We have the shackles, and we have the scepter."

Something invisible brushed along Pia's arm. This time, instead of being freaked out by it, she felt oddly reassured. "And we have the seraphim, for whatever aid they can lend to us."

Dragos met her gaze. "Let's go get our son back."

Chapter Ten

D RAGOS ASKED MORGAN, "Are you coming with us?"

The sorcerer smiled. "Absolutely. I'm with you to the end."

Dragos handed the scepter back to him and shapeshifted into the dragon. Pia and Eva climbed onto his back and after tucking the scepter into his pack, Morgan kissed Sidonie and followed.

Springing into the air, Dragos wheeled to arrow along the coastline. He flew so fast and hard the wind whistled in Pia's ears. Eva's muscled body spooned hers from behind, providing warmth and stability.

"Look behind us," Eva shouted in her ear.

Pushing her hair out of her eyes, she looked. The air was filled with winged Wyr who followed them. They could not match the dragon's speed and rapidly fell behind. "What are they doing?"

"They're going to war with their Lord," Eva told her. "Their demesne was attacked, and their children are threatened. They were all just waiting for Dragos to act."

To make the choice to go to war against one of the

dragons was a very brave thing to do. If it came to them actively fighting, many of them would die. While she smiled at the sight of their loyalty, she hoped they would not arrive in time.

Eva carried the shackles on her back, and she was touching Pia. Did that mean they would affect Pia too? She tried reaching out to Dragos telepathically. *Where are we going? Are you still able to contact the sentinels?*

Most people's telepathic range was no more than ten feet at best, but Dragos's range was more like a couple hundred miles. And apparently she was far enough from the shackles, because Dragos replied, *Yes. Graydon said he flew to a bluff and landed briefly at the top, then launched again and came this way. He stopped to retrieve his scepter.*

Now he knows it's missing. Pia narrowed her gaze as she tried to think like an evil megalomaniac. Senusret had to know his scepter hadn't been stolen by a random thief. His impromptu hiding place was too remote for that. *And he knows we have it. His level of desperation just went up.*

He's also not experienced with using Liam's body. Graydon said he's not flying as fast as Liam or I can normally. The sentinels are keeping him in their line of sight pretty easily.

She shivered, glad for Eva's strong arm circling her waist. *If they can see him, he can see them which also rachets his desperation higher.*

Not necessarily. They're cloaking their presence. He knows he'll be pursued, but he doesn't know they're right on his heels. Feral satisfaction ran like a bright red river through his voice. *He's making for the closest crossover passageway. And he also doesn't know that I've got guard stations on both sides of the two passageways.*

Her stomach clenched. She was growing tired of that feeling. *They don't know that Liam is compromised. They'll let him through, and then he could go anywhere.*

That's not going to happen. We'll catch up with him before that. But just to be sure, I've asked Khalil to go ahead to both stations and warn them. He paused. *Khalil just told me the children were at the station under Malan Wei's protection. He's helping to evacuate them now to another safe spot.*

Her brief flash of alarm at his words quickly abated. This was what life with Dragos was like. While she was busy concentrating on the moment, he constantly ranged far and wide, talking with multiple people, often all at the same time, and playing strategic chess.

It was something he enjoyed, and he was superb at it. As far as she knew, the only people who ever gained his complete attention were her and the children, and only then when there wasn't a crisis going on.

Or when they were making love. She was one hundred and ten percent certain she had all of his attention then.

Surely her chess master would know what to do next. Her telepathic voice filled with hope as she asked, *What are we going to do when we catch up with him?*

He was silent for far too long. Then he replied, *I don't know.*

Hope withered like a fragile flower. Balling her hands into fists, she pressed them to the dragon's bronze hide.

That wasn't what she wanted—needed—to hear.

After twenty-five miles or so of following the edge of the sea, Dragos veered away in a new direction. She recognized the route. It was the same one they had taken when they had flown to the settlement from the crossover passageway. A short time later, magic shimmered as Dragos threw a cloaking spell over them.

Morgan, who had been silent until that point, said from behind Eva, "We're getting close."

Pia's breath shook. Yes, they were close. And Dragos didn't know what they were going to do.

Her own words came back to haunt her. The only way Senusret was going to leave her son was if he was forced to.

They either had to find some way to kill Senusret, or he has to believe Liam is going to die.

No pressure at all.

THE WHITE DRAGON came into Dragos's line of sight. He was still a few miles away, but Dragos could see the steady, plodding nature of his flight, the measured rhythm of the rise and fall of those massive wings. None of it looked instinctive or natural.

How had Senusret accessed Liam's Wyr side? Did it cost him to maintain control over it, as he maintained control over Liam's consciousness?

He sincerely fucking hoped so. The more tired Senusret became, the quicker this confrontation would go.

Up ahead, at a bend in a river, the sentinels had gathered to wait for their arrival. Dragos said to his passengers, "Hang on."

A few moments later, he sloped into a downward descent. Whenever he had passengers, he had to fly like he was driving a Honda minivan so he didn't dislodge anyone, and right now he burned to shed that restriction.

Once he landed, Eva and Morgan slid to the ground, but Pia didn't. Dragos waited a heartbeat longer, then he told her, *You need to get down now, lover.*

I don't want to, she whispered.

He felt badly for her. *You can't go with me for this next bit. Just like I couldn't go into the seraph's realm with you.*

Sometimes I hate it when you're right, she hissed. She leaped off his back. "I need a gryphon!" Then, as all three gryphons stepped forward, she said, "Not Graydon or Rune. Bayne, you're not mated. Will you take me up?"

"Of course." Bayne crouched so that she could climb on.

"We're still going with you, cupcake," Graydon sounded annoyed.

"No, you're not," Dragos said. "None of you are. You've tracked him this far. You've done your jobs. The more of you who are involved at close quarters, the more opportunities he has to possess someone else. Stay back a good half mile."

Since soul repositories were not something he had experience with, he glanced at Morgan for confirmation. Morgan nodded. "I think that should be safe."

Pia looked grim and terrible. She was blood streaked, her clothes torn and grass stained, hair tangled and missing a sizeable chunk at the back. She was, now and always, the most beautiful thing Dragos had ever seen.

"Give me the shackles, Eva," Pia said.

The other woman looked furious, but she handed the backpack over. Pia shrugged it securely onto her shoulders and belted it to her waist.

Morgan strode to Bayne and Pia. "You need me. Like Dragos, Senusret can't possess me if I'm on guard against it. Not even while I hold his scepter."

"Fine," Dragos bit out. While he appreciated everything that Morgan had done so far, every decision led them into needing to trust Morgan further, and he didn't like extending so much faith on a largely unknown entity, especially over something so important.

Morgan leaped onto Bayne's back.

Dragos didn't wait for further discussion. Freed from constraint, he shot upward and lunged through the air at his son. Every wing beat brought him closer.

The cloaking had worked for them so far, but at some point Senusret would hear the thunderous beat of Dragos's wings.

Or would he?

Dragos doubled down on climbing in altitude while still working to overtake the other dragon, going higher and higher until he could look down at the sunshine glinting off Liam's white hide. As he strained to gain the position he wanted, the weight of a body settled on his back, at the juncture where the base of his neck met his shoulders.

Awareness of who had joined him chilled his bones. *I don't want you here.*

Get over it, said Azrael. *We have flown together many times before, and you know we will again. Besides, you may need me.*

My son is off limits to you, he growled. *Do you hear me? You cannot have him.*

You know that's not how this works, Death replied.

Live or die. Kill or be killed. It was the only rule in the animal kingdom. Every herd, pack, lone predator, and species that developed venom and adaptive coloring knew the code.

As the Great Beast, Dragos knew it better than anybody, and most of the time he was just fine with it. Most of the time Azrael didn't bother him in the slightest, and sometimes Dragos invited him to the battle.

But sometimes he hated Azrael with all his heart. Azrael was the one person he could not outrun or outfly, the one person he could not block from entering a room. If Dragos threw him off his back, Azrael would simply appear at the scene in some other way.

But dwelling on old resentments wasn't going to free Liam. Setting his resentment aside, Dragos kept an eye on the white dragon below while he waited for the right moment. Counting the passage of time in his heartbeats. One, two....

The white dragon stretched out his wings to glide for

a few moments, giving those powerful shoulder muscles a break before he resumed the hard work of flight.

…. There.

Folding back his own wings for maximum velocity and extending all four feet with talons outspread, Dragos plummeted. He dropped from the sky with the speed of a small airplane. Several tons of force slammed into Liam's back. There was no room for error. Even as he struck the other dragon, he grasped hold of the juncture where Liam's wings met his body and broke the bones with a resounding snap.

You're not flying anywhere with my son's stolen body ever again.

The white dragon screamed. The sound trumpeted through the sky. Dragos mantled, trying to brake their downward fall, but the other dragon struggled so violently, he flipped them end over end, and together, white dragon and bronze, they plunged to earth.

The force of their impact drove outward like a bomb, leveling trees and stamping a deep crater into the ground. The breath drove out of Dragos's body and one of his hind legs snapped. Straining to move at his top speed, to drag the air back into his aching chest, he twisted in a gigantic roll and came to his feet.

He couldn't put weight on his broken leg. It felt like it was on fire. Pain was pain; it wasn't death. Ignoring it, he brought his focus onto the other dragon and readied for battle.

Lying in a twisted, awkward position, the white

dragon convulsed. *Liam*. With a leap, Dragos straddled the other dragon's body. "Come on, son!" he roared. He searched the white dragon's blue eyes for any sign of Liam.

Recognition flashed across Liam's face. He half-growled, half-gasped, "Do whatever you have to. Just get him out of me!"

Then that brief glimpse of Liam vanished, and the white dragon began to laugh breathlessly. "Really, Dragos, what are you going to do now?" Senusret asked. "He's the ultimate hostage… and you can't pry my arm away from his neck. I'm killing him from inside—you know I can—if you want your son to live you have to let me go…."

Rage and terror paired flawlessly together, like the world's most poisonous wine.

"I already told you once," Dragos snarled. "I don't negotiate with terrorists."

Snaking his head down, he closed his jaws around the white dragon's throat and squeezed. Liam's hot blood filled his mouth. The white dragon fought, raking Dragon's underbelly with those long, razorlike talons. Bright, hot pain filled Dragos's mind.

He clenched down harder. Leave him, you bastard.

Pia, Morgan, and Bayne raced into view.

"He's going to disembowel him." Bayne dove to wriggle between the two straining dragons. Somehow, mostly, he got those raking talons to stop digging into Dragos's belly.

Get ready, Dragos said to Pia.

Get ready to heal him.

She still wore the backpack with the null spell shackles. She couldn't have possibly heard him, but she crouched near their heads.

"I'm here." Pia sounded clear and steady. "Liam, if you can hear me, Mom is here. Everything is going to be okay. We're going to get you safe."

If I kill my own son, she'll never forgive me, he said to Azrael. *She might want to, but she never will. I'll never forgive myself.*

Azrael knelt by Liam's head. He laid a hand on the hard jowl. "They are fighting inside. You can't let up."

The hot sun beat down. Gradually, the white dragon's struggles grew weaker.

Morgan pulled out the scepter and held it in front of the white dragon's eyes. "Senusret, you have another choice. You don't have to die with Liam."

"Get out of him, you monster!" Pia screamed.

The raw pain in her voice. Closing his eyes at how unendurable it all was, Dragos squeezed his jaws tighter.

"Dragos may not negotiate with terrorists, but I do," Morgan said, his voice filled with alluring, seductive Power. "If you leave him, we can get you a body. Perhaps a coma victim will do, or maybe a baby who doesn't have a personality formed yet. You won't have to struggle all the time just to stay alive. Think of the possibilities, Senusret. Life is right here waiting for you."

"And so is Death," Azrael said. "This is your only

choice. There will never be another."

The white dragon stopped moving.

No.

Something subtle and invisible flowed out of Liam's body.

Azrael straightened from his crouch. "I've got him now."

Rearing back his head, Dragos roared, "*WHO DO YOU HAVE?*"

Pia collapsed on Liam and sliced her hand open with a pocketknife. She must have cut deep, because her blood flowed freely and fell into the gaping wounds at Liam's neck. "Come on, baby," she sobbed. "Stay here with us. Liam, I beg you. Don't leave me."

"They're both gone," said Azrael. "No—wait."

Dragos wanted to claw at the world. "Wait for *WHAT?*"

Death smiled. "I have never seen so many seraphim before. They have Liam, and they're bringing him back."

As they stared, the wounds at Liam's neck began to heal. Nausea hit. Dragos managed to shapeshift into his human form and roll off the white dragon before vomiting violently. He retched, spat, and retched again, fighting to get the taste of Liam's blood out of his mouth.

His useless leg and the long, raked wounds along his abdomen were a fiery agony. His throat burned with stomach acid, and he couldn't see anything for the tears that sprang from his eyes and streamed down his face.

Kill or be killed. Live or die. This was life at its ugliest, and he would take it.

He would take every painful, stinking, puking, bloody moment of it.

Because his son would live.

Chapter Eleven

ONCE PIA WAS absolutely fucking certain that yes indeed Liam was healing, and her baby was breathing on his own, she left his side to race to where Dragos half-sat, half-lay hunched over, one arm wrapped protectively around his middle.

He looked ashen, wrung out, one leg twisted awkwardly. She eyed with dread the foamy red vomit nearby. "How bad is it?"

Glancing at her and then at the vomit, he shook his head. "That looks worse than it is. I accidentally swallowed some of Liam's blood. My right leg is fractured in a few places, and there's this."

When he lifted his arm, she stared at the deep gaping wounds that scored his washboard stomach. Wet exposed muscle glinted in the sunlight.

She couldn't take her eyes from it. "Bayne? I need help here!"

A shadow fell over her, and Morgan crouched beside her. "Bayne and the other sentinels are inspecting Liam's wings to make sure the bones healed properly. Will I do?"

She gave him a wild-eyed look. Morgan stared at her, his own eyes wide with wonder. He had already proven that he was a very smart man. Realization was another sinking feeling in the pit of her stomach.

Oh gods, not another one. The more things happened and the more she healed others, the more people came to know the secret of her Wyr form. At the rate they were going they might as well post an announcement in *The New York Times.*

Despite the pain he was in, Dragos must have realized it too. He turned his killer look onto Morgan. She gripped his shoulder, digging her fingers into the hard muscled flesh. "Don't do anything rash. He has helped us every step of the way."

"I understand now why your Wyr form is such a mystery." Not very many people could stare their own death in the face with as much calm as Morgan showed. He said steadily, hazel gaze fixed on Dragos, "I swear by the life of my own young king, dead now for so many years and whom I loved like a son, that I will never betray your secret."

The truth rang in his words like a clarion. Pia heard it plain as day, and if she had, Dragos must have too. But it was still a long taut moment before he gave a small, grim nod of assent.

Immediately she slipped an arm around his neck and helped to ease him onto his back while Morgan turned his attention to Dragos's twisted leg. "I'm sorry, but this is going to hurt."

"Do it." Dragos's mouth was white. He stared up at the sky. "Pia, if you're going to heal me, you need to do it fast."

She had seen enough battle wounds to know that his, while difficult and painful, were not life threatening. "What do you mean, *if* I'm going to heal you...." Her voice died away as she noticed the direction of his attention and twisted to look up.

In the distance, a rapidly growing cloud of avian Wyr winged toward them. Oh, shit. The good, loyal Wyr who had followed them to battle were about to arrive. There must be a hundred or more.

Morgan looked too, briefly, then turned back to Dragos's leg. Bracing one hand on Dragos's hip, he asked, "Ready?"

"Yes," Dragos bit out.

With a powerful flex of his shoulders, Morgan pulled the leg straight and aligned the broken fractures. Dragos grunted and closed his eyes. The pain had to have been excruciating. Frantic to finish the job, Pia asked, "Is it good now?"

"He's ready."

She placed her bleeding palm over the wounds on Dragos's stomach, and she and Morgan watched in silence as the wounds knit together into a seamless whole.

Dragos grabbed her wrist. He said to Morgan, "I need your shirt."

Morgan didn't waste time questioning him. Instead,

he stripped it off and handed it over. Long fingers flashing rapidly, Dragos wiped Pia's hand and bound it, then tried to cast his own healing spell over her.

Goddammit. It didn't take.

"Take off the backpack!"

Eyes flaring with realization, she stripped off the pack and dropped it to the ground. Dragos tried a healing spell again, and her cut smoothed over.

Once he was sure that she was no longer bleeding, he scrubbed her palm, then his own abdomen, and asked her, "What about Liam's throat?"

She looked at the white dragon where the sentinels had swarmed over his giant form. "I don't see any blood. I think someone washed him."

"I took care of it. He's clean," Rune called out without looking up from his inspection of one massive wing that Aryal, Quentin, Bayne, and Graydon moved carefully back and forth, extending it out and folding it back into place. Avian Wyr typically did not survive irreparable damage to their wings. Liam's broken wings had healed when Pia had healed his throat, but they hadn't set the bones first and they were taking no chances.

Dragos put pressure on Pia's wrist. Obeying the wordless prompt, she sat back. He held his fist with the bloodied shirt away from her, and his Power flashed. The shirt caught fire. He, Pia, and Morgan watched as the flames engulfed Dragos's fist. The fire did not die down until the shirt had fallen into ash.

Pia said to Dragos, "I need you to be okay now, baby."

"I'm okay." Propping himself up on one elbow, he gave her a quick, hard kiss. "Go check on Liam."

Leaping to her feet, she raced over to the white dragon. Part of her sensed the seraphim, one on either side, who came with her. In those few brief seconds, her racing thoughts gave her all kinds of doom-filled scenarios.

Kathryn Shaw, the talented surgeon who had saved Aryal's wings, had mated with Oberon, the King of the Dark Fae, and now lived two Other lands away.

When Kathryn had worked on Aryal, she'd had to rebreak the malformed injury, and Pia had helped to heal the harpy afterward. Even if they could get Kathryn here as quickly as possible, how on earth could she do surgery on such a giant patient? Pia's imagination stuttered. It would take cranes or something to lift those giant wings and hold them stationary.

She skidded to a stop by Rune, who had placed both his hands on the juncture where one of Liam's wings met his shoulder. "How bad is it?"

He shook his head slowly. "His wings are quite perfect." He looked up and met her gaze. "He was lying on one of them while it was broken, out of alignment, and then healed. I don't think this is scientifically possible."

She stood still, staring at Liam, while her ragged breathing gradually slowed.

Hop. Ta-da. Jazz hands.

The seraphim had caught Liam's soul and given her not only one miracle, but two.

She whispered, "*Thank you for the life of my son.*"

Something faint and gentle brushed along her arm.

A FEW MOMENTS later the avian Wyr arrived, and they had come prepared for the possibility of a protracted battle. That meant, along with carrying all their weapons, the larger ones had also brought snacks.

They passed canteens of water and jerky around, which Dragos, Eva, Morgan, and the sentinels consumed hungrily. Pia didn't begrudge them any of it, but avian Wyr were meat eaters and there wasn't anything suitable for her to eat so she had to content herself with drinking her fill of water. As refreshing as it was, she'd only had a few bites of food before Senusret had grabbed her, and hunger was beginning to make her feel hollow and lightheaded.

She settled in a sitting crouch, leaning against the unconscious white dragon's cheek, and dozed in the hot sunshine while the others milled about, talked together, slapped each other on the back, and said congratulatory things. Dragos was off somewhere doing whatever Dragos did after battles.

Darkness fell over her. Rousing, she opened her eyes. Dragos knelt and held out his hands. He had borrowed someone else's shirt—the scent told her it was Graydon's—and it was filled with wild berries and edible greens: dandelion, chickweed, and fennel.

"I knew you wouldn't leave him. This is the best I could forage on short notice."

It looked like a banquet to her. "Oh, thank you." She fell on the food and ate every piece of green, every berry.

It wasn't enough, just like the jerky wasn't enough for the others, but it would do for now. She felt her energy return. He laid a hand on her shoulder. "We'll eat properly when we get back."

She nodded. Just then, the white dragon shimmered and disappeared into Liam's human form. Rolling to her knees, she leaned over him and stroked the blond hair back from his strong face. "Open your eyes, honey. Everything's okay now."

Raising one hand, Liam groped for hers while he opened his eyes and stared at the sky. Like his father, he didn't need to squint when he looked at the sun.

When he didn't say anything, she asked, "What do you remember of what happened?"

His gaze shifted to hers. "I remember fighting him and Dad pinning me down. And I remember my wings hurt."

His expression was so empty. She had never seen him looking quite so fragile. "Your wings are fine," she told him strongly. "You're perfect in every way. You will fly again just as soon as you feel up to it." She wasn't sure how seraphim miracles worked, and their dragon bodies were so heavy, so she added, "We'll get you examined by a proper Wyr doctor, because you might need to wait a month or so like Aryal did. But there's nothing wrong with them that time won't heal."

His gaze clung to hers as his lips shaped one silent word. Promise?

Bracing one hand on the ground, she leaned down to press her lips to his forehead. "You, Dragos, and Niall are my heart. Would I ever lie to you?"

A sigh shook out of him, and he relaxed. "Never."

As she straightened, she caught sight of Dragos watching them. The bitter self-recrimination in his expression jolted her. He strode away. The open, affectionate love that shone between father and son was missing.

Frowning, she fell into troubled thought.

People began to head back to the settlement. They left in twos and threes, then in greater groups, until finally there was no one left except Morgan, Eva, the sentinels, and Pia, Dragos, and Liam.

As tired as Pia was, she had a debt to repay and a promise to fulfill. With a sigh of relief, she strode over to Graydon and finally relinquished control of the backpack with the null spell shackles. "Don't let Aryal have these again."

"Oh, I won't. I guaran-damn-tee you that," he promised with feeling. The last time Aryal had control of them she had lied and said she had dropped them in a volcano. While that had worked out to their advantage, nobody was about to trust her with them again.

Pia looked around. Dragos was talking to Grym and

Quentin, and Rune and Bayne squatted by Liam, who had sat up and was stretching his shoulders. She was painfully aware that Liam and Dragos had not spoken directly to each other since Liam had regained consciousness.

She could only fix one thing at a time. And right now, there was no time like the present for evening the scoreboard.

She pulled Morgan aside. "I need the scepter now, please."

He raised his eyebrows, but obligingly opened up his pack. "I was hoping to study it. It's imbued with a magnificently unique Power. What are you going to do with it?"

Reverently she gathered it up and held it in the crook of her arm like it was a baby. "I need to take it back where it belongs. If Dragos asks where I've gone, tell him I needed a private moment in the woods and I'll be right back."

Speculation filled the sorcerer's narrowed gaze. "Are you sure you don't need some company for…wherever it is you're going?"

He was too smart, that one. She gave him a lopsided smile. "I'll be perfectly safe. And I also don't need to have a long, drawn-out argument with Dragos over this."

The corners of Morgan's eyes crinkled. "I'll tell him you needed a private moment. If he asks."

"Thank you."

As she walked away, Eva fell into step beside her.

"Where are we going?"

Mentally she rolled her eyes. She couldn't even pretend to take a pee by herself when her warrior Wyr got riled up. "Just keep quiet and follow me."

They walked until the voices in the clearing faded away. Then Pia paused, set the scepter on the ground and shapeshifted into her Wyr form.

Waiting seraphim surrounded them, shining like stars in the woods. By the mystified look on Eva's face, Pia could tell that the other woman couldn't see them.

None of them stepped forward. Changing into her Wyr form had taken her part of the way, but not far enough. She told Eva, *Don't call for help. Just wait here.*

Bending her neck, she picked the scepter up with her mouth and walked forward. The forest scene around her shimmered and faded.

Rhyacia disappeared, and she stood again in the seraphim's realm. Saw again the Tree, and the Dancer.

One seraph approached. Gently, she laid the scepter in its waiting arms. Then she turned to bend one knee in homage to Taliesin. As the Dancer whirled, she could have sworn she saw them smile.

Her promise was fulfilled, the debt for the life of her son repaid.

She turned and headed back home.

Chapter Twelve

EVA AND THE surrounding woods reappeared. The other woman's eyes were wide. "You disappeared. What the righteous fuck just happened?"

The seraph's realm was still too personal for Pia to talk about. Maybe someday, but not yet. She shapeshifted back into her human form and slung an arm around her best friend's shoulders. "Never mind that for now. It's a story I'm not yet ready to talk about. Eva, I am not merely done. I am really most sincerely done."

Eva slipped an arm around her waist. "Okay, but you've got to tell me someday."

Maybe she would, but maybe she wouldn't. Occasionally some things happened that needed to remain private. As they walked back to the others, she asked, "Do you still have that pup tent you use when you go camping?"

"Of course."

"Can I borrow it for a while, along with your bed roll?"

Eva squeezed her. "Anything you want, baby girl.

Just ask, and it's yours."

When they reached the others, the avians changed into their Wyr form and took on passengers. Pia touched Dragos's shoulder. "Are you okay for flying?"

His bleak expression lifted somewhat, and he nodded. Good enough.

Liam rode Rune, Eva settled behind Pia in her usual spot, Quentin and Bayne paired up, and this time Morgan hitched a ride on Graydon. They flew back to the settlement in a casual formation. Nobody pushed it. There wasn't an emergency any longer. Dragos flew in silence, and Pia let him.

They each took turns landing in the clearing by Hell House and changing into their human forms. Mates reunited, hugging each other tightly, and people came up to Pia to hug her too. She patted Bel on the back, gave Carling a brief smile, and said to Eva, "Would you be so kind as to set up your pup tent and bed roll in some shade down at the beach?"

"Of course, right away." Eva was beginning to look worried, but she loped off to do it.

"We have fresh food waiting inside," Bel told her.

No doubt they did. Pia nodded, and the other woman seemed to take it as acknowledgment and turned her attention back to her mate, Graydon.

A few minutes later Pia slipped away and walked down the path to the beach where Eva was just finishing with the tent set up. The bed roll fit perfectly inside the pup tent. Pia touched Eva's hand in thanks, crawled inside the tent, and pulled the flap down. Then she finally, finally let her body go prone. Finally let go of the interminably long, horrid day, and the relief was indescribable. Listening to the waves, she began to drift off.

She felt him approach rather than heard him. When Dragos wanted, he could move as silently as a cat. The tent flap lifted, and he looked inside. "What are you doing?"

"I live here now," she told him. Her limbs felt weighted with lead.

He gave her a fierce frown. Liam peered over his shoulder, looking baffled and worried. Dragos said, "My shoulders don't even fit in there."

"I know." A giant yawn cracked her jaw.

Dragos ordered, "You need to eat and drink. And you're filthy—I know you're exhausted, but you'll feel better when you're clean. Get your ass out here."

She contemplated that for, oh, maybe a split second. "No."

"*Pia*," he said between his teeth.

"Don't you 'Pia' me in that tone of voice, mister. I will not put foot inside that house again. I won't eat or drink anything there, I will not shower, I will not rest there. I will not wear a single stitch of clothing from it, I will not use the toothpaste. I reject that experience entirely, and I don't care if that doesn't make sense to anybody else. All that matters is that it makes sense to *me*. And I'm so goddamn tired I could lie here and die."

At those last words, his expression tightened. He put a hand on her head and stroked her hair. The hair she had left, anyway.

She continued, "So since we don't have a house I can stand to be in any longer, this is my house now. If you don't like it, go do something about it. You're richer than Croesus." Looking beyond him, she added to Liam, "And you can lift a million tons with your little finger."

Reluctantly, one corner of Liam's mouth notched up a fraction of an inch. "Maybe not a million tons."

"You know what I mean." She loved them both so much. But everybody had issues, and whatever was going on between them, they would have to work it out for themselves, because she couldn't fix one more thing. Hopefully, they would take the prompt and work on the project together and get past what happened. If not... She closed her eyes again. Her voice wobbled as she told them, "I need to sleep, and I need my baby. That will be all for now. You may leave."

A taut silence greeted that. She wasn't surprised. She'd never behaved like this before. Then, Dragos said to someone, "Get her food and drink. Lots of calories, liquid, and fat."

Someone raced off, probably Eva. Pia lay still, not caring.

He leaned into the pup tent as far as he could and pressed his lips to her mouth. "You'll get your baby, and we'll have a new place for you to stay by nightfall. I promise."

She believed him. She fell asleep.

The next thing she knew, Eva was there, shaking her awake. Eva held a straw to her lips. "Don't bitch at me. I don't care how tired you are. Wake up and drink this."

She sucked on the straw. It was a refreshing cold smoothie, filled with coconut milk, fruit, and greens. She got half of it down before falling asleep with the straw in her mouth.

Someone shook her awake again. She didn't open her eyes. "What does a girl have to do to get a nap around here?"

Niniane said, "We have your hell baby."

That made her eyes pop open. She reached out with hungry arms. Niall screamed at her. She gathered him close. "Oh, sweetness, I'm so sorry."

Tearfully, Niniane told her, "We never let him cry it out. Someone was always available to lavish love on him, and when they couldn't take it any longer, they handed him to someone else, and Hell Baby. Never. Shut. Up. He drank every drop of milk you sent, so I don't think it was trauma, I really don't. I just think he was really mad."

"Are you my precious Hell Baby?" Pia crooned at him. Niall screamed louder. As she unbuttoned her bra, she told Niniane, "Thank you for everything."

"You, and he, are so very welcome. But I gotta say, I'm really scared about having my own baby now."

As she bared her breast, Niall latched onto her nipple, drew a couple sucks, then pulled away to yell wordlessly at her before latching on again. Both she and Niniane began to laugh.

Pia told the faerie, "Nothing could possibly be as bad as Hell Baby, so I'm sure you'll do just fine."

Niniane slipped away, and after Niall finished feeding, he and Pia fell asleep. At some point a very warm dog wriggled into the tent. Skeeter alternated between putting his chin on Pia's ankle and panting, and between the baby and the dog's added warmth, she quickly grew clammy and uncomfortable, but she didn't have the heart to send the dog out and nobody was taking her baby away again, so she curled onto her side and dealt with it.

When she next opened her eyes, she heard the sound of canvas ripping. Dragos lifted away the top of the tent. "You just ruined Eva's pup tent."

"I'll get her another one." He gathered her up, baby and all, and carried them down the beach. "We got your new house done. It's very temporary."

"I don't care. I'm sure it will be wonderful." She'd almost told him earlier she would be happy with a cave, but she hadn't wanted to lower the bar too far. She looked around blearily. The heat of the day had eased, and the sky was filled with the brilliant colors of sunset. In the distance, she could hear drumming. "What's that noise?"

"Some people decided they wanted to have a real beach party. No weird, dangerous ghosts invited."

"Good for them."

He had showered and shaved, and he wore a pair of khaki shorts. His short black hair was still wet, and he smelled so good it made her realize just how rank she was. "I'm so stinky you shouldn't be touching me."

"I will always want to touch you," he told her. "No matter how stinky or cranky you get. If you want, I'll roll in the mud with you."

"Now, there's true love." She snuggled against his chest.

His arms tightened. "How's the baby?"

"He's perfect in every conceivable way, but he's really mad. He might yell when he wakes up again." She peeked at Niall's tiny, exhausted face. "Hopefully he wore himself out and won't wake up for a while." After a moment, she asked, "How are you?"

He stopped walking to kiss her. "Better. I took Liam to a Wyr doctor, who confirmed his wings healed just fine. To be on the safe side, he still wants Liam to avoid flight for a few weeks. Then he and I got to work on your new place. It was—strange and difficult at first. I—" He stopped talking and the pause turned excruciating. Then, from the back of his throat, he forced out, "I killed him. I killed my own son."

"Put me down," she ordered.

His arms tightened jealously. "No."

"Then look at me." For a moment he resisted, then he met her gaze. The anguish in his eyes made her heart constrict with compassion. "You didn't kill him. You saved him."

"I understand what you're saying," he said carefully. "But my visceral experience says otherwise. I bit into his throat. His blood filled my mouth. He stopped breathing, and his soul left us, and he's only back through the kindness of others."

This was so difficult. It might be one of the most difficult things they had ever gone through, and they had gone through a lot together. She lay a hand against his cheek. "What did he say about it?"

"He said, 'Thank you.'" Dragos gave her a bitter smile.

She breathed through that and let her gaze wander over the beautiful scenery. Then she said, "You know, sometimes, things don't magically get better. Things happen, and we have to endure the experience, and then we need to leave them in the road where we found them and move forward. He loves you so much. He said 'thank you' because he's grateful, and I am too, because you saved him. And I am so sorry that you had to pay the price by going through that experience. But I am so glad and grateful you are strong enough to take this hit and move on. You won't let that monster hurt our family anymore."

He closed his eyes and tilted his head down to her as he listened. "No, I won't. He doesn't get to do that to us."

That was when she knew they had turned a corner, and things would be better now. Maybe not all at once, but day by day, moment by moment, they would be.

Every happy experience they shared, every kiss, every holiday with family and friends, every sunset, and every joke took them further away from Senusret and made him irrelevant.

Dragos resumed walking. "Anyway, Liam and I ended up spending the day together as we worked on this. It was good. And word got around, then people started showing up with donations, and I hope you like what we came up with."

She pressed a kiss to his collarbone. "I already told you. I know I'm going to love it."

She was getting tired of being carried, but she thought he might be enjoying himself, so she put up with it. He rounded a bend, and then in front of them, a gigantic, magnificent tent came into view. It was different from anything she had ever seen before, with several peaks at the top. Warm light spilled out from a spacious opening.

"Oh…" she breathed as she took it in.

"It's fashioned after a Bedouin tent," he told her. "The roof is waterproof, and you can roll up the sides. It will be cool in the daytime, warm at night, and dry underneath. We have rug hangings to delineate rooms, and more rugs on the floor. People gave us furniture, and you have all kinds of new clothes. They were happy to help. They know what you did for them. If Senusret had been allowed to go unchecked, things would have gone very badly here." He cocked an eyebrow at her. "Were you serious about the toothpaste?"

Toothpaste? What was he talking about? She drew her brows together, then remembered and gave him an abashed grin. "I've slept since then and am feeling a bit more sensible."

"No need. We have new toothbrushes and toothpaste too. I was just curious."

Finally at the edge of the tent, he set her on her feet, and she handed the sleeping baby over to him and walked forward wonderingly, staring at the Elven rug hangings and sophisticated Dark Fae furniture. There were couches, and a low table made of burnished wood with cushions set around it. It was every bit as spacious as Hell House had been, with room for guests.

"We've only got one bath area set up," he told her, as he followed her. "And I'm afraid it's a bit primitive. Liam constructed the shower—it took him a couple of hours. There are slats underneath that you can stand on so the water can run through, and wooden sides for privacy. There's warm water."

"How?"

"The Demonkind encampment had some solar heating camping bags they could spare. You fill the bags up, set them in the sun, and when the water's warm, you can hang the bag on a hook and use a nozzle for a spray. Like I said, primitive, but effective." He shook his head. "Technically it doesn't follow the rules, since the bags are made of plastic, but since they already brought them in I decided we should make use of them."

"I love it, I love all of it." It was all completely

different from the things that had furnished Hell House, new and even luxurious, and filled with a sense of their new community. Turning back to him, she beamed.

He smiled. "The guards are here too. I had them set up a ring of tents some distance away. But, we should be a bit quiet if we want to be private. If you want to cook something yourself, you'll have to grill over an open fire, but otherwise we'll have meals delivered. There's food waiting for you in the ice chests."

"I want all of it. Honestly…" She bit her lip as she confessed, "Hell House was wonderful. It really was, and so thoughtful, but I hope you don't mind. I think I like this better."

His smile deepened. "I think I like this better too. It will do very well for now. I enjoy the sound of the waves."

"Me too. Okay, I have to get clean now." She hesitated, looking at the baby.

"Go," Dragos told her. "I've got him."

She was still very tired, so she showered, washed her hair, and brushed her teeth with the spare economy of someone who wanted to go horizontal as soon as possible. She didn't ache. The seraphim had been too generous for that. But she was looking forward to a good night's sleep in Dragos's arms.

After showering, she used two mirrors to check the back of her head. For something that was so painful, there actually wasn't that much hair missing, just a chunk low in the back. She was pretty sure nobody would be able to see it when her hair was dry. And her hair grew fast.

She slipped on an oversized T-shirt meant to fit Dragos and in her new nightgown shimmied happily to the bedroom area. Rich patterned pillows and blankets covered a king-sized mattress.

Dragos lay stretched out, Niall resting on his chest. He rested with his eyes closed, but as she approached he opened his eyes and looked at her. He gave her a slow, sexy look. "Looking good, lover."

Hop. Ta-da. Jazz hands.

Laughter suffused his expression. "Holy gods, I love you, woman."

She fell to her knees at the edge of the bed and crawled toward him. "I might be kinda crazy about you too." He lifted one muscled arm in invitation and she gladly cuddled against him. "I want to be on vacation. Can we just live in a tent by the water and be on vacation for a while?"

He exhaled slowly, eyes narrowed as he contemplated the roof of the tent. "Let's negotiate. Define vacation. By the way, Liam's going to stay for a couple of weeks until he can fly back to the crossover passageway on his own. He's out enjoying the beach party now."

"Yay for us, and good for him!" She bit back a yawn.

"And the sentinels stayed to help us for a couple of hours, more to socialize than anything else, but then they had to go back to New York. They said they had been gone long enough and to tell you they were sorry they didn't stay to say goodbye."

"Totally understandable. I heard them talking about reports and investigations. I'm sure we'll see them again soon." She yawned again. What would a vacation mean to Dragos? And how much could she wiggle out of this negotiation? "I want to go swimming with you, and I want to make love under the stars. I want to look up from a good novel and see you relaxing." She rolled her head on his shoulder to look at his hard profile. "But I also don't want you to feel trapped into doing nothing. Just—let's have fun."

What was she even trying to say? She pushed her lower lip out and pinched it with her fingers. Nation-building, managing different factions of the community, dealing with politics, breaking up the occasional fight between demesne representatives, building their permanent palace high over the water—all of that was fun to Dragos, and this whole land was his playground.

"Maybe I just miss you," she confessed. "Maybe I want your whole attention on me for a little while. I guess I'm not over what happened."

"Pia, it's only been over for a minute. Of course, you're not over it." Moving carefully, he set the sleeping baby to the side. Then he rolled over onto her, pinning her with his weight, and laced his fingers through hers and looked deeply into her eyes. "I always miss you. I never stop thinking about you or wanting you. It doesn't matter what else is happening. You're always at the forefront of my mind. I never knew what loneliness was until you came into my life and taught me what it was like to love someone."

"Yes," she whispered. "I can't stand it when you go too far away."

"I can't stand it either." He kissed her cheeks, her forehead, her mouth, her throat. "I hated that stupid little pup tent."

A snort exploded out of her nose.

He gave her a lopsided smile. "But I do know now why you did it. Thank you for knocking Liam and me together."

"Well, I didn't know if it would work. And my shitfit was sincere." She sniffed and raised her head to kiss his collarbone. "But you're welcome."

He stroked long, hard fingers down her torso and slipped them underneath the end of the T-shirt. He was a master of fire, raising it along her skin wherever he touched, and she gasped and arched as it pooled between her legs. "A week. Just you, just me, and the baby. And Liam whenever he wants to be with us. How does that sound?"

"It sounds heavenly," she whispered. She let her fingers dance across his skin. "Late breakfast, cups of coffee in the shade."

"Naps," he said against her breast. "Very quiet naps, so no one else can hear…."

"Yes, please."

"Morgan and Sidonie are going to stay for now. He

and Graydon are going to supervise the excavation of the rest of the sinkholes, just to make sure there aren't any other dangerous artifacts."

"How lovely for them, but they need to leave our bedroom now," she told him.

His chest moved in a chuckle. "I only meant that doesn't need my attention."

"Oh, I see! Well, then, I approve." She slipped one hand between them and unbuttoned the waist of his khaki shorts. "What else do you want to tell me, my love? I want to hear everything you have to say. For years, and decades, and centuries upon centuries."

"Everything I have to say will be I love you, just in different words and different languages, for the rest of our lives."

Two "I love yous" in one night. That was quite a bonanza from Dragos, who didn't say the actual words very often. Gleefully she hugged them tight.

"I am the richest, luckiest woman in the world," she whispered.

Gently he parted her legs and pulled open his shorts. His beautiful cock spilled out, turgid and large. She took hold of it with both greedy hands, and he hissed. Then he eased inside her and they rested together that way for a while. Lowering his head, he breathed in her breath, exhaled into her mouth.

Sharing breath, sharing life. And when they moved together, it was the oldest, most primal, best dance in the world.

Everything was in motion. Nothing stayed the same.

She paid homage to it.

And how they danced.

Epilogue

THE DRAGON FLEW into New York and landed at the top of Cuelebre Tower. Striding down to the penthouse, he poured two scotches. He left one on the table, took one for himself, and walked over to the ceiling-high windows to look out over the city. The lights of New York at night were endlessly fascinating.

This was his city now. His to claim, his to rule. His birthright, given to him by the father who had killed him. And he would rule it with such savage efficiency the whole world would take note.

The penthouse door opened and closed. He didn't look around. There was only one person who knew he was here.

"Thank you for coming," Liam said.

"You're welcome," Azrael replied. Liam watched Death's reflection as he picked up the glass of scotch and sampled it. "How's life after death?"

Liam finished his scotch and set the glass aside. "It's something to savor."

"And how are you feeling about what happened?"

He turned. Azrael watched him, his green gaze

inscrutable. "I feel chagrined, to be honest. No matter what I did, or how I fought, I could not shake Senusret's grip on me."

"Try not to take it too hard. Senusret had a vast amount of experience in committing his crimes. Not very many people could have shaken him off."

"My father did."

"Your father is—exceptional, and far, far older than Senusret was. And even some of the first generation of the Elder Races might have fallen prey to Senusret's machinations."

"I will never fall prey like that again," Liam said. "And that brings me to why I asked you here."

"I did wonder."

"I want you to teach me everything you can. Every spell, every trick, every way there is to kill somebody. Nobody will take this city from me. And I figured there was no better person to ask than you." Liam's hard blue gaze was rock steady. "Will you do that for me, Uncle?"

Death smiled. How nice to be asked to participate in the development of the next generation.

"Sure," he said. "Why not?"

Printed in Great Britain
by Amazon

81557881R00102